CAPTAIN AMERICA

THE NEVER-ENDING BATTLE

CAPTAIN AMERICA

THE NEVER-ENDING BATTLE

ROBERT GREENBERGER

JOE BOOKS LTD

Published simultaneously in the United States and Canada
by Joe Books Ltd, 489 College Street, Suite 203, Toronto, ON M6G 1A5

www.joebooks.com

Library and Archives Canada Cataloguing in Publication
information is available upon request.

ISBN 978-1-77275-212-0 (print)
ISBN 978-1-77275-213-7 (ebook)

First Joe Books edition: November 2017

MARVEL

Printed and bound in Canada
1 3 5 7 9 10 8 6 4 2

*For Joe and Jack, Stan and Jack, Steve and Sal, Roger and John,
Marc, Ed, Mark, and all who helped create and
sustain the symbol of liberty since 1941.*

Private Steve Rogers was just one man among many filing into a small boat. He looked no different from the men on either side of him. Well, that was not entirely true: Rogers was broad shouldered, muscular, blond-haired, blue-eyed, and handsome in a movie-star way, although few noticed that about him given his frequent absences and low-key personality. Still, the gruff, jowly sergeant took particular pleasure in yelling at the man, mocking him for having the company mascot, James Barnes, hanging around him like some pet dog. Rogers always looked ahead and never reacted to the shouts and taunts. When asked to drop and give the sergeant twenty, he did so with ramrod precision. When asked to peel potatoes while on KP duty, usually for missing a bed check or roll call, Rogers nimbly worked his way through the pounds of spuds, amazing the cooks.

"Get a move on it, yer goldbricks," Sergeant Duffy shouted.

While this should have been motivating, it wasn't, the troops under the command of Sergeant Mike Duffy having heard that phrase so often it had became background noise. While normally the soldiers would move into formation anyway, the severe African heat proved wearing on the men. More than a few felt seasick as they moved in the small landing crafts headed for the shore. Currently attached to the 3rd Infantry Division, Duffy's men had been hastily put on a boat and shipped from the United States as part of thirty-five thousand troops moved aboard one hundred ships. Once in Africa, a place not a single member of Duffy's squad had ever visited, the division was placed under the command of Major General George S. Patton. En route, it was explained to the young, nervous men that the goal was to secure the region from the Vichy French in order to launch a campaign against the Nazi army, commanded by Erwin Rommel. Patton and Rommel had both grown in stature as legendary warriors in the spreading global conflict—to serve one and attack the other was a tall order for men who had been training and stationed in Virginia mere weeks before.

To Rogers, putting up with Duffy and missions like this one was part of the price he paid for being the symbol of America. Less than two years ago, he was identified by General Chester Phillips as something special, even though Rogers had been a ninety-eight-pound weakling, considered too frail for armed service. The Lower East Side–bred eighteen-year-old desperately wanted to serve his country, knowing full well the conflict in Europe would sooner or later reach across the Atlantic and drag the United States into the war. So when Phillips asked him to be a part of the military's Operation: Rebirth program, he said yes.

Since then, he had served multiple roles, more than he had expected. There was, of course, the military uniform of the army, which he wore with pride. But in his red, white, and blue uniform, he was Captain America, the country's living symbol of freedom, designed to counter Nazi Germany's own embodiment, the garish Red Skull. As Captain America, Rogers initially toured rallies and recruitment drives, was flown to England as a sign of America's support to their beleaguered ally, and occasionally routed saboteurs on both sides of the Atlantic Ocean. To provide cover and additional combat training, Steve Rogers was finally admitted into the army, assigned to Camp Lehigh in Virginia, close enough to the War Department that he could come when summoned, but protecting his alter ego from the watchful Sgt. Duffy proved more challenging than contending with the fifth columnists.

Soon after Rogers donned the colorful uniform, Barnes—nicknamed Bucky—discovered his secret, so Rogers trained the streetwise teen and recruited him as his partner. While that doubled the challenge on missions, the lean, brown-haired youth proved a worthwhile addition. Their friendship was forged quickly and held tightly, regardless of how dangerous their assignment was. Bucky also reminded Rogers that wearing the uniform and meeting the likes of President Franklin Roosevelt and Prime Minister Winston Churchill—and yes, punching bad guys—could be fun.

The fun was on hold for now. The first Americans had arrived in England that January, but this would be the first time soldiers would be used in a major offensive, Operation Torch. Assigned to Patton's Western Task Force, the 2nd Armored Division and the 3rd and 9th Infantry Divisions were about to land in Morocco. Most of the men had to look at maps to figure out where they were going, having barely heard of the place. Rogers' group was part of the smallest, arriving at Mehdlya-Port Lyautey as part of Operation Goalpost, a subset of Operation Torch, with orders to secure the port as part of the overall objective of taking North Africa back from German control. Crammed tightly aboard a rolling vessel, they were headed for the beach just as the sun was beginning to peek above the sandy horizon, painting the sky in light, pastel shades of yellow and orange. The men chewed gum, regripped their rifles, kissed their crosses—anxiousness diluting the normal chatter.

Barnes leaned over and whispered, "What do you think about this big deal being called Operation Torch? Think it's named after our mutual buddy?"

Rogers shook his head knowing Allied Command was not in the habit of naming missions after the super-powered beings aiding the effort. In this case, Professor Horton's remarkably lifelike android, the Human Torch, was stateside and not at all a likely consideration.

"It was originally called Operation Gymnast," Bucky said with a chuckle.

Rogers turned, his eyes wide in surprise. "Where'd you hear that?"

"You know us mascots, always getting underfoot, always eavesdropping when no one is looking. You'd be amazed at what I get to hear. Maybe you influenced them."

Rogers didn't think so, although he was well aware that President Roosevelt and his secretary of war, Henry Stimson, always knew where Steve Rogers was located, even manipulating his entire division's orders to place Captain America where he could do the most good. Since this would be the US Army's first major assault, they wanted their symbol to be present as a rallying point, but notably at the smallest of the three operations. Rogers had had Bucky sneak their uniforms aboard the tiny vessel in a duffel bag, ready for an opportune moment.

Right now, though, Rogers felt like every other grunt making his way to shore—a little nervous, a little excited. It was one thing to take on threats in chain mail while carrying an indestructible shield; it was quite another to be charging into battle with only a rifle and a helmet for protection.

"Why us?" Joe Esposito groused beside Rogers. The darker, black-haired man had joined Duffy's group just before boarding the ship.

"Because we're Americans, dummy," Gary Kowalski,

on Esposito's other side, whispered. "The Frogs hate the Limeys, but like us Yanks. With us attacking first, they're less likely to open fire."

"Makes sense," Esposito agreed. "But, geez, we're sitting ducks out here."

Rogers wondered about that, hoping there was a reason there was no aerial covering fire softening up the Vichy defenses as the boats neared shore. They were just a hundred yards away, and the action was about to begin.

"Look sharp," Duffy said, using his *I really mean it* tone. "Safeties off and move on my command." There was a chorus of metallic clicks amid some murmured prayers.

Several boats were gliding to a stop against the soft, damp sand exposed by the receding tide. Soldiers poured overboard, splashing and sucking sounds accompanying every footstep. As they hit the land, there was no immediate enemy fire, emboldening those who followed.

Duffy's unit reported to Captain James Rosenthal, who, having just arrived on shore, was consulting his map. As Rogers' boat came up behind Rosenthal, Rogers could tell the captain appeared confused. Duffy jumped over the side in a smooth move belying his bulky form, and hurried over.

"We're not in the right spot," Rosenthal bellyached. "The formation broke up and clearly the *Savannah* sent us in the wrong direction. We need to regroup, and fast. Sergeant, begin formations."

Rogers had noticed he was beginning to sense when things were wrong, a sixth sense warning him of danger. When he had described it to Stimson recently, the secretary suspected it meant Rogers was developing heightened tactical senses, along with all his other gifts, formed through his experiences as Captain America. The super-soldier formula clearly not only enhanced his musculature, but his brain functions as well. As a result, he'd begun to trust those feelings, which had yet to let him down, so he waggled his fingers at Bucky, signaling to indicate they'd be in their other uniforms sooner rather than later, his eyes already scanning for safe cover in which to change. Nodding in acknowledgment, Barnes shifted a box of grenades and took out the bulky duffel bag, slinging it over his shoulder.

In the distance, Rogers spied the stone fort at Port-Lyautey, knowing the French within would soon be alerted to their presence. The boxy, buff-colored structure reminded him of the castles of old Europe, seeming incongruous here in Africa.

The beach offered little protection and even less privacy for the two to change outfits. About 150 yards to their right was a stone outcropping that would obscure visibility; it would have to do. All he needed was a distraction so they could fan out with the troops, then disappear. The mayhem of battle usually allowed them to move unseen.

Rosenthal was hailed by a boat motoring into view, and Rogers looked over to see another commanding officer. Later, he'd learn it was General Truscott going from misdirected group to misdirected group, personally relaying a delay in the attack from 0400 to 0430. Washington was unaware of the delay and had already announced the commencement of operations to the media back home, so whatever element of surprise the invasion possessed quickly evaporated.

Sure enough, as the American troops advanced, the Vichy French in the fort opened fire. Men fell over already dead while others dove into the sand or behind rock. A few fell to one knee and took aim, firing back. Gunfire filled the air, drowning out the rhythmic waves lapping around them.

Joining the cacophony were heavier roars from the coastal batteries and the buzz of French warplanes heard between shots.

Rogers looked around and took in the scene. There was more confusion than precision, and the errant landing seemed to have unnerved someone up the chain of command, who had issued erratic orders. His fellow combatants were pinned in spots, but there were enough scattered men that he and Bucky would not be noticed.

At a sprint, he and Bucky made a beeline for the outcropping. At first, they paused to take position and open fire. Then, as return fire neared them, they ducked out of sight, seemingly for protection. They'd have to hurry, hoping no one noticed Rogers and Barnes had dropped down while Captain America and Bucky appeared. Both men had gotten very good at being quick-change artists and were soon in their primary colors, masks in place.

Bucky retained his rifle while Captain America avoided gunplay at all costs. In Rogers' mind, there was a place for such weapons, but his mission had to be about ideals and symbols. Despite being a country founded on armed conflict, America was first an idea, and he hewed to those notions.

"Stay behind me," he commanded, and then crawled up the rock to gain some height and avoid connecting his arrival with Rogers' disappearance. Once they were about ten feet off the ground, they scrambled over the outcropping and into view, the shield reflecting the rising sun. They made their way over the rock and to the ground, charging directly toward the fort. Rogers hoped his bright shield would become a target, saving the men. Running on uneven rock and soft sand was difficult, but as the land hardened, he gained momentum. Around him, men noticed the costume and shouted his name or let loose whoops of joy. He had to grin at that, but never slowed down or acknowledged the cheers. There was a mission to complete.

The shield vibrated as bullets struck it time and again. Rogers had long before gotten used to the sound of impact and ricochet. He raced toward one of the 25 mm guns, manned by two soldiers. He let the shield slide down his arm, his hand grasping the edge, then flicked his wrist and the precision throw found its target, slamming into the pair before curving around to return to his outstretched hand. In all, it took seconds, leaving him exposed, but no gunfire came his way. It didn't hurt that Bucky was a step behind him, laying down covering fire.

They worked in silent unison, Bucky following Captain America's lead in the heat of battle, arguing tactics afterward. The sixteen-year-old brimmed with ideas and a headstrong desire to work on his own. Cap dissuaded him, but he knew how determined Barnes could be, and soon he would need to let the boy stretch. Now, though, was not the time. There was still the fort to attack and more men to disable.

Those men were concentrating their fire in front of him as well as at him, bullets kicking up gouts of sand and dirt. He could hear soldiers firing from behind along with a few commands about following his lead, which wasn't exactly his idea.

"Bucky, flank right," Cap ordered. Without a word, his partner veered off, away from the increased gunfire. The shield would hold as the impacts rattled his arm but not his nerve. Instead, he increased his speed, pulling ahead of his fellow soldiers, and neared the fort, an imposing stone edifice with flat sand before it. He drew close enough to make out the French fighters in their drab earth-toned uniforms. One was taking dead aim at him, close enough that if the shot bypassed the shield, he'd be hurt.

At the crack of the gun, he executed a forward roll, compacting his form and moving out of range of the bullet, which harmlessly impacted the soft ground. Rising to his feet, he hurled the shield at the enemy while still running. It smashed the rifle from the surprised man's hands and effortlessly returned to Cap.

By this point, Cap was close enough that he was a difficult target, allowing him to scramble up the side of the fort, grabbing at the trim for leverage at each level. His sandy boots slipped on the rough, aged structure, but his superior strength allowed him to make it up. He swiveled his hips and leapt onto the fort's roof, stunning a soldier in the process.

Using his shield as a battering ram, he plowed through the half-dozen men, all swearing at him in French. The tone told him all he needed to know as he knocked three off their feet with one blow. His right fist pummeled a fourth soldier while the remaining two reached for him. Each soldier tried to grab an arm and hold him, but they were no match for his strength.

"*Mon capitaine,*" one man called, trying to distract him, but Cap shrugged and another of the men was thrown from his side into the caller. Another swung his legs from the concrete floor, trying to knock Rogers down. Instead, Cap wrapped the man's legs between his own, then threw himself to the ground, yanking upward with his legs—a wrestling move he'd been taught back in high school, where he could form the move but lacked the mass to make it successful. Now, the strain on the Frenchman's body was intense.

While they were both on the floor, the other soldiers rallied and tried to stomp on the American. His shield once more protected him as he untangled himself from the lame man and rose. He was taller and broader than any man there, his muscles practically dancing under the blue and white sleeves. He gave the men a wolfish grin, intended to intimidate; it seemed to work as one, then another, dropped their weapons.

"Ha!"

Cap took several steps backward and then risked a sideward glance, seeing Bucky, rifle aimed at the men, now atop the fort with him.

"We need to secure them, then move downstairs."

"Way ahead of you, Cap," his partner said, grabbing a French flag and ripping it into strips with the pocketknife he carried.

Watching Bucky at work, Cap reflected that this was their first taste of true combat. He hoped he had saved Duffy and his comrades. More ships were approaching with thousands more American soldiers coming to take control of the port near Casablanca. He and Bucky would disappear, letting the US and British armies get full credit, while Rogers and Barnes would rejoin the soldiers for whatever mop-up work was required.

Captain America had gone to war, but this would be far from his last battle.

CHAPTER ONE

The wheels grinding against the tarmac woke Steve Rogers from his sleep. He'd been dreaming about French snipers in Africa during the last hour of the long-haul flight. He hadn't thought about that fight in a long time. Or of Sergeant Duffy, dead all these years. Surrounded by the congressional delegation, he was stretched out on a recliner in the airliner's first-class section, comfortable in a sport jacket, dark-red button-down shirt, and gray wool pants. It was more curiosity than a sense of duty that had led him to agree to accompany these politicians. It had been decades since he'd set foot in some Eastern European countries, and he was interested to see how much they had changed. Still, he hoped his presence wouldn't upset their status quo. It was one of the reasons he had been hesitant to accompany the delegation when he first saw the itinerary—while physically Rogers appeared to be in his thirties, the super-soldier serum and fate conspired to prolong his life, and he'd first visited Transia and Slorenia during the Second World War.

Weeks ago, when the secretary of state had invited Rogers to Washington, he'd told Rogers people still remembered all that Captain America, Bucky, and the Invaders—along with the American troops—had done to liberate them from the Axis powers. Rogers' participation would be seen as a good-will gesture, ensuring positive press at home and abroad, along with providing the congressional team an extra level of security, not that there was any threat they knew of, Rogers was told, but they had been surprised in the past.

People were stretching, turning off various devices, and finishing their drinks. They were here to tour a quartet of countries to see whether trade could be improved between any of them and America. Finally, these smaller countries were trying to establish their own destinies, a goal he could appreciate. After all, it's what he and the Allies had fought to preserve. Too often since then, he had been reactive and felt unable to chart his own course. Then again, that was the life of a soldier, which is how Steve Rogers still saw himself. There were others who saw him as the living symbol of the American Dream or of the country itself, but these days, there were so many differing ideologies that no one definition of America or the dream it represented was definitive. Instead, Captain America had to stand in the broadest terms for the resilience, innovation, and determination that had allowed the original colonists to cast off the shackles of an indifferent ruler. On this trip, he was representing 350 million people who collectively were known as the United States of America.

"I really need to adjust my fantasy lineup before the meetings begin," Christopher Gallo complained.

"There should be some time before the first session," Gabby Lewin said. She and Gallo were the two aides selected to accompany the four members of Congress.

"Good, because I saw one of my guys went on the DL just as we took off," he said. "Man, I hope I brought my adaptors."

"Can't help you with that, I need mine."

"And that they have Wi-Fi."

"We're traveling to another continent, not another century," she shot back, a winning smile on her face.

"But these tiny Balkan places might have crap service."

"Sucks to be you." Lewin laughed, her tone feisty and playful. She turned to Cap, "You have a good nap?"

"I certainly did," Rogers told her.

"We're being cleared by the Symkarian military and should be deplaning shortly. You might . . ."

"Freshen up?"

"Suit up," she said. "Our press and their press will be expecting someone in chain mail, not a blond Adonis in a coat."

Changing into his uniform in the tiny bathroom would be impossible, so Lewin escorted him to the galley, where the flight attendants admired him before being shooed out and the curtains were drawn. He made quick work of the change, and was soon ready to do his part.

Gallo got off his phone and gave everyone a thumbs-up. "We've been cleared and the king is already here. You've met him before, right?"

"Yes, briefly," Rogers replied. "It was a quick in-and-out visit. There wasn't much time to chat."

"No, you just swooped in, saved his life from Sabretooth and Solo, then took off with Spider-Man and Silver Sable to finish the job," Lewin said, her admiration clear in her voice.

"Really, dude, you did all that?" Gallo asked, impressed.

Rogers didn't like talking about himself, even though he'd had to do it since first stepping onto a battlefield during the Second World War. As far as he was concerned, it was one thing to swap war stories with Nick Fury or wounded soldiers at first aid stations, but it was another to use his exploits as entertainment. It felt like he was glorifying his efforts and making himself out to be more than he was—at least that's what he believed, even if he was alone in that assessment.

"More or less," was about all he would admit. The reality was that he had arrived in Symkaria to help stop the mercenaries from killing the king. Unfortunately, once that was done, he'd needed to accompany Symkaria's champion, Silver Sable, and Spider-Man on a global manhunt. He'd always meant to come back for a visit, but the next time he returned he was leading a team of Secret Avengers as they prevented an arms dealer named Voydanoi from freely operating in the country. That anecdote was way beyond the security clearance of wide-eyed congressional staffers. He'd wanted to stay and explore the country, but circumstances had once more called him and his operatives away.

"Were you here during the war?" Gallo asked, thankfully changing the topic.

"No, it was one of the few places I managed to miss while on duty," he said. He knew the tiny Balkan country had suffered great losses keeping the Nazis off their land.

"Their PM, Tartaryn, insisted we arrive here first," Lewin said, her distaste evident.

"Martinez made a big deal out of that, preferring we start in Slorenia, but quickly came around," Gallo said.

"Yeah, he's become our mother hen, a real stickler for the schedule," Lewin added. "Wish he was that focused on the details back home."

"Does it creep you out to be so close to Doom?"

"What a dumb question," Lewin shot back. "It's not like the country's about to be invaded by Doctor Doom or his Doombots or anything like that. They're more allies than anything else. You were at the same briefings I was in—how do you not know this?"

"I remember Latveria and Symkaria formed an alliance

to forestall the Cold War from disrupting their rebuilding," Gallo huffed. "But that was the 1950s, and Doom's here now."

"Rest easy, Chris," Cap told him, clapping his red-gloved hand on the man's shoulder. "Doom's been keeping a low profile, as has Prime Minister Lucia von Bardas. There's little advantage in disrupting this meeting. He's left Symkaria alone all this time; that speaks volumes. Doom is always after the big game."

Rogers knew that with few natural resources, Symkaria's economy was in free fall, and drug trafficking emboldened the local underworld, complicating Parliament's ability to take control of the engines of business, such as they were. Neighbors or not, they were, frankly, beneath, Doom's notice.

The Symkarians were a proud people, Rogers recalled, and didn't want to appear to be beggars, but they needed help. He wondered what the United States could offer in trade that would make the delegation interested in helping. Captain America recognized that his presence meant a larger than usual press contingent, and if that would help these people, he was fine with that.

His musing was interrupted by a flurry of activity in the rear. A door had been opened, allowing the press to hit the ground first, and letting them set up to capture the formal arrival and meeting with King Stefan.

"Captain, if I may…" a soft voice said. He looked to his right and saw one of the attendants holding up a cloth. "You, ah, have a spot on your shield."

He grinned and nodded, turning so the red, white, and blue shield faced her. She splashed something on it then gave it a vigorous buffing.

"Much better," she said.

"Thank you. We all have to make a good impression, don't we?"

He was used to such public appearances, and the pomp and circumstance surrounding them. He'd campaigned for war bonds, the Red Cross, Toys for Tots, and countless other causes over the years, posing for thousands of photographs (selfies they were called now, he reminded himself), and cramping his hand after just as many autographs. The out-pouring of affection bolstered his spirit and reminded him of all the good he could do without resorting to his fists.

"It's time, and we have a schedule to keep," Congressman Thomas Seaver said, consulting his ever-present tablet.

A shaft of light flashed to Cap's left as the main cabin door opened and a rolling ladder was placed from the outside. The four members of Congress lined up in seniority order, something they'd squabbled over as the airplane crossed the Atlantic before Cap fell asleep. They would emerge first, then Cap, followed by the two aides, and finally the flight crew. State had worked with them on the choreography of the events and had established the itinerary, although no member of the office accompanied them. Cap could hear a band and cheers even before Roberta Ojeda, the senior member of the team, stepped out.

She was tall and elegantly dressed, carried herself with dignity and a serious demeanor, and had spent the flight buried in reports and correspondence, never smiling. Gripping the railing, she let it slide through her hand as she descended the steps followed by Seaver, Al Jackson, and the rookie, Pedro Martinez. They made for an interesting quartet—a mix of ages, genders, and nationalities—a microcosm of America itself, Rogers considered. There was the tall, stately Ojeda; the wiry, curly haired Martinez; the tall, graying Seaver; and the dark-skinned Jackson, his face weathered and his hair almost entirely gray.

"We don't botch this trip," Seaver said, "and it could mean millions for these countries and better trade for us back home."

"Ensuring your re-election," Martinez said.

"Eyes front, lips zipped," Jackson admonished his junior colleagues. Out of respect for him, they obeyed.

Cap paused out of sight of the crowds, letting the elected officials have their moment before he stole the spotlight. It was far from intentional, but he knew being a symbol made him a magnet for attention—and danger. His senses switched to alert and he listened, then took a deep breath.

Everything felt appropriate, nothing out of the ordinary, for which he was grateful. With luck, the entire eight-day trip would be nothing but meet and greets, too much chicken, and lots of interviews.

He silently counted down from ten; at one, he stepped into the sunlight. The midday air was warm and pleasant, a picture-perfect spring day. Cap saw that the delegates were already shaking hands with several dignitaries, including Prime Minister Tartaryn. The band was moving on from the Symkarian anthem to something folksier, but they were nearly drowned out by the cheers of the throng contained far from the plane yet close enough to spot the Star-Spangled Avenger. Cap gave them a wave, and then slowly descended the stairs. As his crimson boots touched the ground, members of the local press swarmed past their security handlers to get their close-ups, shouting questions in a mix of Symkarian and English. Most were asking how the country looked nearly seventy years after his first visit—clearly, their research was faulty, or someone had misled them. He patted the air before the press, indicating he'd talk to them soon enough.

Walking by them, Rogers strode purposefully toward the other Americans. Ojeda made a gesture and introduced him to the prime minister. Tartaryn was a little shorter than she was, although he tried to puff himself up to close the gap. His dark, charcoal-gray suit was expertly tailored for his trim build, and his red-and-white-striped tie was held in place by a gold clasp featuring the country's flag. Quickly, Cap saw him as flash over substance, unwisely spending more than a few Symkarian francs on appearances.

"Welcome back to our country, Captain," he said in heavily accented English.

"My pleasure. I'm glad I will finally get to see the country rather than taking a quick trip through."

"And to try our *galips*," a deep voice said from the side. Cap turned to see King Stefan, accompanied by Silver Sable, striding toward them, ignoring the congressional delegation.

"Galips," Cap repeated in a questioning tone as he and the king shook hands.

"Think jelly doughnuts," Silver Sable said with a smile. "Small in size, potent in sugar."

He chuckled and noticed she was wearing full combat gear in her trademark white and silver. From the snowy hair to the leather boots, she was a shapely column of white, and armed to the teeth with visible and no doubt hidden weapons. Although they'd battled together in the past, they barely knew one another.

The king was beginning to show his age, laugh lines around his mouth, crow's-feet around his dark eyes. He was tall and fit, preferring a Western suit to traditional attire. He looked good—nowhere near as ostentatious as the prime minister.

"I must have you taken to where the best galips can be found," King Stefan said. "It is the least I can do for the man who saved my life."

"He had a little help," Sable said, frowning.

"Ah, yes, from that amazing Spider-Man," the king said, shooting Cap a wink.

Taking the initiative, Rogers steered the king toward the delegation and made the introductions. Hands shaken all around, the king beckoned the unimpressed prime minister then signaled an aide who ushered the press over for the requisite photo op. As that was occurring, Captain America and Silver Sable drew back from the cameras, taking a moment to talk.

"How are things here?"

"Quiet," she said. Like him, she had been on alert, and even now her hard, blue eyes were always in motion, sweeping the airfield. Her accent was far less pronounced than the others, thanks to her international work with the Wild Pack, her highly trained militia. He also knew her Silver Sable International was the country's major revenue generator, preventing its people from falling destitute.

"You mean we get to relax this time?"

"Maybe you can," she shot back. "I have a king to protect. I don't trust Tartaryn at all."

"Your country hasn't had many productive PMs, I gather. What's the problem?"

"Tartaryn is all about us being too small, our size is hindering our progress. It's not like we can buy up other land. We have to deal with what we have, which is why Stefan needs your country's help."

"Is there something Symkaria can offer America? Other than you, of course."

"I'm not for sale," she said, her voice flat.

"You know what I mean," Cap said, thankful he wasn't leading the trade talks.

"King Stefan believes we can be a distribution hub for the region, helping identify the best trade routes, clearing customs and the like."

"An entire country as middle man," he mused.

"Something like that," Sable said. "Even if it puts a few thousand people to work, that would help. It's all he has. It's been such a strain, and we've never had it easy—for decades that's been the case."

He could hear not just the pride in her voice, but also the strain the responsibility for carrying it on her shoulders had. Cap did not envy her.

A rumble and flash of bright, yellow light in the distance interrupted the conversation. Battle-trained senses had both super-heroes change posture, crouching back to back, scanning the cloudy, blue sky. They swiveled their heads toward a second flash of orange-yellow light to the east.

"That's the castle, the capital!" she called. "Damn, I don't have my jet pack."

"I'm on it," Captain America said. "I need a car!"

He looked around the airport and spotted a motorcycle leaning against the nearest hangar. Without a word, he took off at a dead run, knowing full well Sable's first obligation was to protect her king, and he had no idea where the rest of her Wild Pack were, so couldn't count on them. He was fortunate there were keys in the battered motorcycle's ignition, and he gunned it to life. Aiming toward the plume of smoke, he took off without giving the delegation a second's thought. They were safer at the airport.

One advantage to Symkaria being such a small country was that it was a quick trip to the capital city of Aniana, and he suspected the royal palace itself was under attack. Concussive echoes could be heard and felt above the guttural sounds from the motorcycle's engine, which was protesting the speed he demanded of the machine.

That the attack began shortly after the American arrival could not possibly have been a coincidence. But who was responsible? It was public knowledge the king and prime minister would be at the airport, so what advantage was there in destroying the castle? His keen, analytic mind raced through possibilities, including that this was a trap or a distraction with the king still the primary target. But with Silver Sable on hand, King Stefan would be well protected.

Cap swerved the motorcycle around cars and trucks, several of which honked their horns as a few drivers cheered his highly visible presence. Other drivers, though, were heading toward him at risky speeds, trying to get out of the city. A full panic and exodus such as was underway could be dangerous with the first responders no doubt already at the castle, leaving few to control the masses trying to get away. The city wasn't large, and few of the buildings were particularly tall, so Rogers was able to get the glimpse of twin plumes of black smoke that coiled around one another in the gentle spring breeze. The attack hadn't happened by air, which meant this was a ground-based battle, something he excelled at.

He gunned the motorcycle once more, wishing he was closer so he could identify the attacker. Hearing the bike cough and choke at the constant top speed meant it wouldn't last much longer. Thankfully, he was nearing the beautiful gardens that created a natural barrier between the castle and the city. He could see a red figure up ahead, her hands enveloped in coruscating yellow energy. He racked his brain, trying to isolate which women were so powerful. Given his location, he reviewed European agents of destruction, which led him to the Peristrike Force and its powerhouse, Scattershot. He wasn't sure how she did it, but she could generate destructive energy blasts, each similar to multiple sticks of TNT. He'd have to put her down hard and fast. At his present speed, there was no way he would prevent her from unleashing the blast building up, but at least it appeared aimed at the castle, a two-story stone construction that was once the fortress that repelled barbaric invaders.

Scattershot let the energy rip through the air and Cap winced as the blast shattered stone, brick, glass, and wood, sending debris in every direction. People who hadn't vacated the gardens or perimeter walkways were pelted by the destruction, several losing their footing, others knocked flat to the ground. Movement caught his eye and he saw that whatever security forces were on duty were being rallied by a red-and-blue-uniformed leader, who was packing one of Silver Sable Industries's patented energy rifles. There was panic in the stances of some guards, determination in others. Their leader—a stern-looking man of about fifty, with graying hair and an air of command—gestured wildly in the air, positioning the guards in a semicircular formation, hoping to surround Scattershot. It was a matter of which soldier would be the target, probably dying in the process, but allowing the others to open fire as she recharged.

Captain America was not about to let anyone die. Scattershot was stalking the grounds, fresh energy dancing around her fingers, but there wasn't enough to unleash yet. Cap slowly counted the seconds, gauging her refresh rate and buying time for the bystanders to get out of the way. Wisely, the security leader kept his people from opening fire, allowing more citizens to move away. Still, there were the injured on the ground, who could not move without help, and the guards themselves were likely to be seriously injured if she let loose a blast in their direction.

Cap knew he had to move Scattershot away from the population center. It would come down to a matter of timing since she was focused on the formation around her; among all the chaos she had created, she had yet to notice his approach. He slowed down and ditched the wheezing motorcycle near the old, thick trees that lined the entrance pathway. As he counted and studied the scene, his arms automatically slid the shield from his back and into his hands. Eyes that had seen so much horror and evil measured the distance between his position and the woman, who continued to pace, her hands glowing ever brighter. The white hammer-and-sickle design down the center of her outfit proclaimed her Russian loyalty, while she kept her face covered in a red cowl, exposing just her nose and mouth. Her bare right arm and covered left arm betrayed a lack of muscular tone. If he could get close, he could easily handle her in hand-to-hand combat, disabling her as long as she didn't blast him.

Cap realized she was ready to unleash the fresh discharge as she made her intentions clear: the security guards were her next target. Both hands rose, the crackling energy ready to fly from her fingertips.

He readied his shield, noting it had been about twenty Mississippis between blasts—timing was everything, he had to strike at just the right moment.

He half expected her to boast something before mowing down the guards, who by now had taken aim, ready to fire.

Scattershot extended her arms wide, and he realized she was going to bring them together, the unleashed energy arcing and cutting down the men in a single move.

Tensing, he noted a gentle breeze coming from the east, so he adjusted his position slightly, then, as the air before him grew a fraction brighter, he hurled the shield.

The shield had withstood pounding from the Hulk's fists, and even impact with Mjolnir, the Uru hammer wielded by his comrade Thor. Its superb balance and sharp edge made it unlike any other weapon used on Earth. Now, it sailed through the air with unerring precision at an angle that allowed it to get between the released energy blast from Scattershot's left hand and the soldiers in the blast's path. The shield reflected the energy away from the men, sending it up into the air, scattering what few birds remained in the trees. While he could not stop the right-handed blast, it gave the men a chance to move, and only two were directly hit, their armored uniforms singed black.

Even as Scattershot's attack was thwarted, Cap raced back to the bike. He jumped on and restarted the engine, praying it would work, and was relieved when it kicked up gravel behind him. The motorcycle roared back to life, bringing him closer to his target.

The shield's unexpected arrival rattled Scattershot and

she frantically looked around until she spied the Avenger. A quick glance at her hands showed she was between charges, and Rogers estimated there was enough time to reach her before she could fire again. What happened next was the result of years of experience and his uncanny timing. First, he aimed himself directly at Scattershot, who stood still, anticipating a faster recharge. He shifted the motorcycle's angle slightly so he was heading to her right, and swept her off her feet with one muscular arm as he sped past. Then, he tilted them both toward the ground, adjusting for her weight, as his other hand let go of the handlebar and neatly scooped up his fallen shield. Quickly, he righted the motorcycle and continued roaring forward, through the garden and onto one of the pathways that led toward the city proper.

Scattershot shrieked in frustration, hurting his right ear, as he continued to put distance between them and the castle.

"Sixteen Mississippi, seventeen Mississippi . . ." he muttered aloud as his eyes scanned for a direction away from the people. There were three- and four-story buildings, retailers of all sorts, and an open-air market within sight. None looked promising, and Scattershot's struggling made the cycle wobble. It was already being pushed beyond its design tolerances and soon would give up the ghost, so he needed her handled quickly. Finally, he spotted an alley that appeared to lead to a courtyard.

"Nineteen Mississippi . . ."

He was momentarily distracted by the electrical charge in the air at his side. The sky seemed to be also glowing faintly yellow, and he knew she was going to let loose, risking both their lives as she attempted to escape.

At twenty, he let go of Scattershot and dove to his left, the riderless motorcycle going a few feet forward before wobbling and falling over, belching exhaust. As Cap left the cycle, he tucked into a forward roll then sprang up into a crouch, shield before him.

Scattershot let loose in his general direction, but he was able to absorb the concussive impact as his shield diffused the blast itself. After the expenditure, he snapped upright and confronted the angry woman. Snarling, she muttered curses in Russian, words he hadn't heard since he was at the front during the war. Sparks glittered around her fingers, but there was nothing left to fire at him.

Instead, he got closer and said, "I don't have a way to inhibit your powers, so forgive me." He delivered a left uppercut that clicked her teeth loudly together and propelled her backward, off her feet. She was unconscious before she landed roughly on the cobblestoned courtyard.

Behind him, he heard a rush of boots on the pavement and swung around, shield at the ready, but saw several of the king's guard. Behind them was Silver Sable, purposefully striding toward him. She did not look at all happy.

"The king?" he asked.

"Stefan is fine," she replied. "The Wild Pack operatives still in country are with him now. The king and your Americans are all well protected. What about her? She's Peristrike, right?"

"Scattershot," Captain America confirmed.

"Nasty woman," she said, earning a small chuckle from the Avenger.

"She needs about twenty seconds between blasts, but she can be contained with the right equipment. Does your company have anything like that?"

"No, but S.H.I.E.L.D. is on the way, and they're certain to have that in their armory."

At that, Cap looked up. Sure enough, high in the sky, the unmistakable silhouette of a Helicarrier was breaking through the clouds, reflecting sunlight off its steel frame.

"What did she want at the castle?"

Cap shook his head. "We didn't have time for a proper conversation."

"Too bad, because you'd be nicer to her than I will," she said.

"I don't know about that—after all, I decked her."

"All in a good cause."

As Helicarrier *Crescent* neared, Cap's helmet radio clicked on, and he quickly described the scenario and what was needed. It wasn't long before a transport arrived with several black-uniformed agents, carrying a case. They opened it with silent efficiency and withdrew oval devices that were fitted over Scattershot's hands. One agent activated them from a tablet, and a series of lights flared to life, indicating they were operational. The Russian was starting to come around, and she got as far as pushing herself up with her arms before she was surrounded.

The agents took Scattershot into custody aboard their small transport ship; after Captain America exchanged a few words with the agent in charge, S.H.I.E.L.D. left without fanfare. All told, they were on the ground for fewer than five minutes. By then, though, a crowd of people had gathered around, largely to see the legendary Captain America.

"I trashed someone's motorcycle," Captain America said, jerking a thumb toward the now-silent vehicle. "I owe them some money."

"Autograph it, and he can buy a new one," Sable told him.

"Who in Symkaria has that kind of money?"

"Other than me? I suppose the king. But there are collectors out there, museums that put these kinds of artifacts on display."

"Better the motorcycle than me," he said, his mocking tone belying the truth. On more than one occasion, in his darkest moments, he wondered whether he should be in a museum, on display as a cautionary tale about man's hubris. How many had died as a result of the super-soldier program? There were the test subjects prior to him, and then poor Dr. Erskine, who had died simultaneously with Steve Rogers' rebirth.

The cheering sounds from the crowd forced him to push those dark thoughts away, and he waved in acknowledgment. Cell-phone cameras snapped away; within seconds, this would be global news. It was becoming increasingly hard to keep things under wraps, and he wasn't so sure that was a good thing—there were times news needed to be cultivated and prepared for the world to comprehend as opposed to people seeing unfiltered reports without context. All the world would see was that an American hero had to come to Symkaria's aid—again. After all, it was not that long ago that Captain America and Spider-Man had aided Silver Sable in protecting the Symkarian king. Their national pride had taken a hit then.

An old woman, head covered in a shawl and slightly stooped, had wormed her way forward and was watching with haunted eyes. Cap noticed her but held his ground, hoping a car, or even a bus, would arrive soon so he could investigate the sound coming from the crowd.

"This is how it begins," she said loudly in a thickly accented voice. "They start with the castle, and then they fire on us."

"What are you talking about?" the man beside her asked in Symkarian.

"I was a little girl, but I remember hiding under the bed when the bombs fell. A day later, soldiers could be seen in the forests."

"That was the war," another said in English. "This was one woman."

"All it takes is one," said a younger woman coming forward. "Then another. We're easy pickings."

Captain America couldn't understand all the words, but he recognized the tone. The fear was familiar to him, and his heart went out to the scared people. They were already struggling, and now this attack. Without understanding why Scattershot was there, fear-fueled rumors would run wild.

"We need to contain this before there's a panic," he whispered to himself.

"Go do what you do best." He cocked his head down at her. "Be a symbol of hope."

Taking that as an order, he strode forward and began shaking hands, posing for pictures, and accepting hugs. His actions changed the tenor in a heartbeat, allowing the people to feel joy, even if only for moment.

A fleet of SUVs arrived and Silver Sable helped part the way for the pair of them to leave the crowd before more questions were asked. They were whisked back to the castle, where, they were informed, everyone was waiting. The car ride was silent and thankfully brief. Emerging from the cars, a phalanx of guards formed a clear way for the pair to access the castle grounds. The smoke had thinned out, but was not entirely gone, and firefighters were just finishing hosing down the portions of the structure that had been hit. Police and the high-tech security force had set up barriers with the universal yellow warning tape to keep the curious away.

King Stefan and his prime minister walked slowly through the debris, surveying the damage. Both were followed by their usual aides, but also by two heavily armed members of Sable's Wild Pack. Captain America walked the grounds on his own, crushing stone beneath his boots as he studied the scene. His mind flashed back to other ancient buildings that had been ruined thanks to man's aggression. The sound of cannon fire echoed in his memory as he recalled watching German, Czech, Polish, Sokovian, Slorenian, and Austrian structures that had stood for centuries be wiped away in minutes. The Blitz of London was equally devastating, leaving thousands to cower in backyard shelters or Underground stations. He could easily recall the acrid smell of war, the sounds ricocheting through his memory. When he awoke after decades of suspended animation, he had hoped mankind had learned its lessons, but much like they hadn't learned from "the war to end all wars," the world he woke up in was little better than the one he had left behind. Where man had improved was not in diplomacy and dialogue, but in faster, more efficient methods of creating carnage. While there were no world wars, how many civil conflicts were there? On top all of that, Earth seemed to be a favorite target of alien races—or worse, a prize to be fought over.

Clustered off to the side was the American delegation, milling about in a small, contained space. Cap headed their way, and the group crowded around him. Tersely, he explained who had attacked the capital and where she was. The group frowned at the news, and Seaver tipped his head toward the American press.

"You have to tell them something," Ojeda said.

"Shouldn't it be the king's decision?" Cap asked.

"He'll address his people, his way. We have to assure everyone back home everything is under control. Show strength and resilience."

He nodded once, recognizing an order, even if the congresswoman wasn't exactly in his chain of command. The first to thrust a recorder before him was Harper Simmons, from the *Guardian*. "What happened, Cap?"

Again, Rogers repeated the story, keeping to just the details.

"Are there causalities?" Brenda Swanson asked. She was waif-like and blonde, young to his eyes for such an assignment.

"That's for the king or his representatives to discuss."

"So there were dead?" she pressed, although he noted the horror in her eyes.

"It's clear there were injuries, but I can't speak to the extent of them since I was not there for the full attack."

"Why did Scattershot attack at all?" asked a woman with piercing dark eyes and short, blonde hair. He recalled her name, Melissa Singer, but couldn't remember where she was from. However, he had noticed she didn't seem to get along with the others—not one of the American pack, he gathered.

"That's something we'd all like to know," he admitted.

"She's Russian, so is Symkaria being invaded?" Singer pressed.

"That's highly unlikely. It was just her. Yes, she's Russian, but it doesn't mean she was here on behalf of her government. An invasion by one operative, even one so powerful, would be a foolish maneuver."

"She's solo, then, no evidence of others in the country?" Aaron Amberson asked. He was the veteran reporter in the group, having globe-trotted his way to an impressive career in the Edward R. Murrow school of reporting. Cap liked his work, but tried not to show favoritism.

"She was a member of Peristrike Force, but her teammates have not been seen," he replied.

"Isn't it curious she would choose to attack on a day everyone knew *you* would be here," Singer observed over Amberson's next question.

"On the surface, yes," Cap began, but the reporters shifted their attention, and he had to crane his neck to see why. It was the king himself, coming over to address them. Sable was no more than five feet behind him, watchful.

"On behalf of a grateful nation, I want to thank Captain America for saving lives and minimizing destruction of property." Recognizing a cue, the Avenger turned and shook the king's hand, cameras capturing the moment.

"How badly is the castle damaged?" Amberson asked.

"We're assessing that now, but to properly restore it will be . . . difficult."

At that, Ojeda and Seaver walked into camera range, seizing the opportunity to pledge financial support, assuring the king and the viewers at home that America stood behind the country.

It was a few hours later, over dinner within the damaged castle, that the king and the Americans could speak frankly, without the press, who were dining with their peers in a separate facility. Steve Rogers, in a striped button-down shirt and beige light-wool pants, and Silver Sable, in a white off-the-shoulder dress, were included in the meal and discussion.

King Stefan toasted the Avenger, thanking him once more for his heroic acts. Congresswoman Ojeda toasted the king and reiterated America's support. With the formalities over, a wild-game entrée was presented to the group. The Americans and Symkarians were interspersed to foster conversation and goodwill, so the dialogue shifted topics with speed.

Martinez questioned Tartaryn about Symkaria's iron ore, to which the older man replied, "It's purer than anything in Europe. That's our chief export—other than the Wild Pack."

"Being a small country, are you worried about the supply being played out, leaving you short?"

"Nonsense," Tartaryn said. "We dig deep and leave little to waste. Now, try the bourbon, distilled following an old family recipe."

"I'd rather hear more about the iron—" Martinez pressed. Tartaryn was a beefy figure, looking even larger in contrast with Martinez's trim form.

"Or your jet manufacturing," Seaver interrupted. Cap noticed Seaver had been doing that since they left America, starting on the plane ride. He was focused almost exclusively on high-tech trade, looking for deals to aid his state of Oklahoma.

"We don't have a Stark or Richmond, but I think we make up for that with our manufacturing capacity," the minister said, sipping his own glass of liquor.

"How do they do with altitude?" Seaver asked. "We're always looking for the next generation, getting us closer to space."

"You want altitude, we can design for that," Tartaryn said with a hoarse laugh. "How high do you want?"

Near the king's right hand, Rogers heard Stefan and Congressman Jackson discuss the castle's rich history.

"We're already struggling to maintain routine infrastructure, to be sure," King Stefan said. "The quarry where similar stone has been extracted in the past is nearly played out, too. Our historians will find this a fresh challenge, as will the exchequer."

"There's never enough money to go around," Tartaryn groused, distracted from boasting about the country's jet planes. "We're too small a country, unable to scale up for industry."

"Do you have a theory?" Jackson, a former Major League Baseball player and five-term representative from Arkansas, asked. He was enjoying Symkaria's wine, having already asked for a bottle of his own.

"Not at all," the king admitted, his accented English heavy with fatigue. "We have nothing anyone would want badly enough to destroy and kill for."

"Damn peculiar they struck today of all days," Jackson observed.

Rogers leaned to his left, catching Silver's eye. She shook her head, indicating she had no answer for Jackson's question either.

Prime Minister Artem Tartaryn, in something akin to black tie and tails, looked overdressed for the occasion, since the formal state dinner was not scheduled until the following night. He watched the proceedings with cold eyes, taking everyone's measure, much as Rogers was observing him.

"We may not have much in wealth," Tartaryn said. "But our people make lovely crafts. And Silver Sable International exports some impressive firepower."

"Symkaria cannot entirely depend on one company to

power the nation's economy, even if we are a nation with under two million people," Silver said.

"It used to be our size was an asset—too small to be bothered with," Tartaryn said. "Now, we're too small to compete in a global economy, having just coal—which no one wants anymore—or jets. Other than Silver Sable, our chief export is, sadly, drug trafficking, and only one of those is legal. We need more than that."

"Do you have anyone who can pitch a hundred miles per hour?" Jackson asked with a smile. "Our congressional aide is in need of some help."

Gallo chuckled loudly at that, and gave the congressman a thumbs-up.

"We don't even have a football team," the prime minister complained, taking a fresh glass of wine. "We're too small to even be competitive in sports."

"There are other things we can offer the world," Sable said, trying to turn around the conversation.

"Miss Sablinova, what else do you suggest we export?" the prime minister asked.

Jackson took that opportunity to jump in. With a broad smile, he said, "We'll be discussing that very thing tomorrow morning, but we're here to propose importing, not exporting. We want to put more of those people to work."

"Saved by a politician—what is the world coming to!" Sable said, bringing laughs from those around her. All the while, Steve Rogers was lost in thought, taking the cover she provided and using it to work through what had happened earlier in the day.

It was a mystery, and one that would clearly not be solved that evening. If anything, he knew that the attack would keep S.H.I.E.L.D. nearby, and the extra firepower might come in handy. For all he knew, it was an attack not with a physical goal, but a mental one, designed to scare the Symkarian people and confuse the government, softening them up for something larger.

"C'mere, Cap," a hoarse voice yelled, and the red, white, and blue figure turned to see a thickset man with graying hair. He held a camera in his hands and gestured for the hero to pose with a group of soldiers. Over the last two years, this had become second nature for Captain America as he posed for countless photos and endless newsreel footage. He'd stood beside world leaders, pageant winners, movie stars, and the rich. But he took special delight in being with his fellow soldiers, giving them a respite from the battles that kept them far from home. Regardless of what else was happening, he would always make time for them.

Here, he stood with six other men; from their accents, he could tell they hailed from around the United States. Most were not yet twenty but had already developed a hardened or weary look in their eyes—the result of constant tension, too little sleep, and a fear of death. They'd seen plenty of death, too, since the troops had fully engaged in the war just months before. Rogers had been there for that first attack in Northern Africa, and now he was back, this time lending some moral support to the men, having been summoned days earlier, interrupting a planned mission to Slorenia, when it had become apparent that Rommel, the Desert Fox, had been roused from his den and was stalking the American and British forces.

For a brief moment, he was pleased Sgt. Duffy and the men he trained with were elsewhere, then realized elsewhere might not be any safer. At this point, his services as Captain America were needed far more than those of Private Steve Rogers, so Secretary Stimson had orders cut to reassign several men, Rogers included, scattering them so none were the wiser. Duffy told Barnes to follow Rogers, with the parting words, "He's such a sorry excuse for a soldier he'll need you to look after him and make sure he remembers his rifle every morning."

For this brief visit, Bucky had remained in England, training with the newly founded band dubbed the Young Allies, a gaggle of teen heroes who needed discipline before they could function as a smooth fighting unit. Bucky had seen enough action to know how to turn the young men and women into an asset. With Rommel coming, Rogers was perfectly fine with his partner out of harm's way—this time.

Field Marshal Erwin Rommel had smashed through the initial Allied defenses en route to Tunisia's capital, Tunis.

Now he was headed for the Dorsal Mountains and its two-mile wide Kasserine Pass, backed with seemingly impregnable tanks. General Lloyd Fredendall asked Captain America to make a brief visit to bolster the troops' spirits, even though the general deigned not to join him, remaining at his headquarters eighty miles away. Ignoring the slight, the Sentinel of Liberty visited the First Battalion, 26th Regimental Combat Team, the US 19th Combat Engineer Regiment, and the Sixth Field Artillery Battalion, offering encouraging words, posing for pictures, and signing countless postcards to be sent home. The men were weary, since Rommel's assault had begun on Valentine's Day, and after his initial attack was repulsed, had regrouped and kept moving closer.

Someone's walkie-talkie squawked nearby, and all voices hushed as it was answered. The elation felt moments ago vanished in the thin desert air, replaced with heavy tension. More people gathered around, pressing in around the tall, skinny man.

"The German Afrika Korps battle group is coming!" he cried in a high voice.

Sergeants and corporals yelled orders as men snapped to and followed the commands. For a brief moment, Captain America stood alone, uncertain of how best he could help.

"Fill me in," he demanded of the private, who was clutching the walkie-talkie so hard his knuckles had whitened.

"Germans and Italians broke through the line to the west.

They're climbing up Djebel Semmama. The 10th Panzer Division arrived during the afternoon, and now they're regularly firing, damaging the line holding the pass."

"Sounds rough," Cap mused.

"That's not all," the youngster said, speeding up his delivery and adding specifics, seemingly in awe of talking to the hero. "After failing to take the first line of defense with just armed forces, the Panzer Grenadier Regiment Afrika, supported by the Panzers of first battalion of the 8th Panzer Regiment, arrived and began pounding away at the American, British, and French forces."

Cap already knew that the Allies, settled in the region, were positioned in strong points dug in along the valley floor and adjacent ridges, behind some hastily established minefields, tank obstacles, and wire entanglements. It was those barriers that would prove vulnerable to Rommel's tanks.

"Okay, go find your brigade," Cap said, placing a firm, comforting hand on the man's shaking shoulder. He looked into the private's scared eyes and added, "We've got this. It's what we've trained for."

The private nodded once and ran off.

Cap felt aimless, a new and unwelcome feeling, so he continued to walk from position to position, encouraging the men or helping them move munitions and supplies into position. The work felt good in the cool air, and at least he was making a positive contribution. Morale was low, and so Captain America swung into cheerleader mode, talking up the soldiers' experience and effort, which would make the difference. The men smiled and nodded, shook his hand, and said all the right things, but the look in their eyes betrayed their worry.

By the time the sun had gone down and the cool desert air crept across the land, Cap was sharing coffee with a small cluster of men, swapping stories about their hometowns. They were interrupted by a runner with word that the 19th Engineer Battalion, defending nearby Highway 17, had been overrun. As if to punctuate the comment, the concussive sounds of cannon fire reached them again and again. To his trained ears, Cap couldn't make out what weapon was in use, which concerned him.

He rose, drained the last of his coffee and tossed the cup to one of the men. "What's the fastest way to the highway?"

A sergeant gestured over his shoulder toward a truck. "Get in, I'll drive. Spurrier, you ride in the back." The sergeant identified himself as Curtis, from Pittsburgh. All the men gave their names and instead of rank or serial number, and their hometown. It was a way to find commonality, a way to indicate they were all in this together.

There was a brief scramble, and then the truck was put in gear, kicking up fine grit and gravel as it lurched forward. The radio installed in the truck relayed a message that two companies of motorized infantry, an additional battery of artillery, and some antitank guns were almost in place, which should slow down Rommel's machines of death.

There was another wave of deep-throated gunfire followed seconds later by the impact. Cap expected to feel the ground vibrate and was reassured when things remained steady.

"That doesn't sound good at all," Curtis said.

"Just get me there, and I'll see what I can do," Captain America said.

"It true you really punched out Hitler?"

"Staged, Sergeant," Cap said ruefully. "I don't think it's funny today."

"I'd like a crack at him," the man said.

"Wouldn't we all?"

Before they could arrive at Highway 17, the sounds of battle reached them, punctuated by the loud booming of cannon and tank fire. The darkening sky flared time and again as projectiles and bullets flew back and forth.

Just after 2000 hours, the radio came to life once more, and Cap recognized the voice of the scared private from earlier in the day. "Sgt. Curtis, we have just received orders. All units are to stand or die, no withdrawal unless to counterattack. Over."

Cap grabbed the microphone and acknowledged the command. As the radio fell silent, the heavy clank of advancing tank treads filled the air. "Tell me about the area."

"Highway 17 is considered the eastern corridor, heading toward Tébessa, not terribly wide so the tanks have to go single file," Curtis said. "The 26th Armored is on their way to meet them."

"So are we. When you think it best, stop so I can get out and reconnoiter. You and the private find a group—don't be out here alone and don't try to be heroes."

"Aye-aye, sir. After all, you outrank me, *Captain*. Besides, I'm a grunt with stripes, you're a hero."

"We'll see about that," Cap said, disliking the notion they belittled their service and elevated his own. As far as he was concerned, the tank fire could kill them all regardless of status.

They drove another minute or two, then Curtis pulled the truck to the side of the road, getting out of the way of advancing tanks with Allied markings. Where they were headed was difficult to discern, but if they were here, that meant it was time to get out and do some work. Captain America shook the sergeant's hand, tossed a salute at the private, and left the truck. Staying on the side of the road, hoping the dusty air and night sky would help obscure his colorful uniform, Cap surveyed the scene as he moved closer.

Illuminated by cannon fire, he could make out the silhouettes of multiple tanks, trucks, and men up ahead, all with their backs to him. They had fanned out on both sides of the highway, the path now blocked by numerous machines. Beyond them, in the dim distance, he could just make out the shapes of the enemy ordnance. For him to do any good, he would need to cross to their side and start taking out the tanks and cannons.

An incredibly loud boom resounded just then, a sound more powerful than he was accustomed to, and he saw more than a few soldiers duck down and cower, hands over their ears.

With reinforcements coming from all sides, Cap recognized he needed to slow down the Axis effort and buy the Allies some time. That, he knew how to do. He spotted a cluster of men hunkered down behind a truck, gripping their rifles. They had no one to command them, and their body language spoke of uncertainty.

"Geez, look . . ." one man said.

He was shushed by another until all eyes were turned and a few jaws dropped open. Cap crouched down beside them, hoping they were they only ones who had spotted him so far. There were some quick handshakes, and then the color-fully clad soldier looked over the truck's hood to study the landscape.

"On my mark, I want you all to lay down covering fire," he told them.

"Where are you going?"

"Oh, man, you're not trying to get across the road," another said.

"Like the proverbial chicken," Cap admitted. He focused once more, isolating men and weapons, anticipating the crossing time, and which would be the most likely target. He'd have the element of surprise only once and needed to make it count. Finally, he saw a mortar gun with just two men slightly to his right. He'd start there. Gesturing, he called the men's attention to his acquired target, and they nodded confirmation one by one. The men then spread to either end of the truck and readied their rifles. As they settled into position, each gave a thumbs-up.

Captain America gave the scene one last look, then opened his hand, fingers splayed. One by one, he closed them, counting down.

As the final finger formed the fist, he launched into motion. With every step, he gained speed. On each side, he could hear the covering rifle fire zip past him. His shield was at his side to minimize wind resistance, but his left arm was tense, ready to swing it forward for protection. Since being allowed to actually fight, he had been at first reliant on his superior strength and endurance, but increasingly, he was applying his training, feeling like a more effective combatant.

He could hear more gunfire and then German voices, crying in some alarm.

Before they could fully react, he leapt into the air, arms spread. Like an attacking eagle, he pounced on the two men by the mortar, dragging them to the ground with his momentum. One he smashed against the large cannon, while the other took a right to the jaw and collapsed. Bracing himself against the mortar, he planted his boots and then tipped the weapon on its side. As it fell to the ground, he was already in motion, shield before him as he plowed into a phalanx of men giving him their full attention. There were maybe seven in all, some aiming weapons, others cocking fists. He drove into them, arms and legs flailing, too close for any to get off a shot. The guns now impeded their hands, and he cracked bones and delivered concussive blows. While a few of the Germans landed solid blows, his chain-mail uniform absorbed the worst of the attack.

They might be good soldiers, excellent with pistols and rifles or controlling larger weapons, but clearly, none had been given good hand-to-hand training—in fewer than two minutes, they were down.

Of course, their fight didn't go unnoticed, and more Germans trained weapons in their direction, heedless of shooting their own comrades. There was a dizzying thrill in the air as each fancied himself the one to kill America's greatest hero.

For his part, Captain America was far from ready to surrender, let alone die. Taking careful aim, he hurled his shield, which smashed into three men while he went in the opposite direction and disarmed four more. By then, he was close to one of the tanks, intent on taking it.

One of the Nazis had collected the shield and tried to turn the weapon against its owner. It sailed forward four feet then crashed into the ground, letting Cap scoop it up and clamber up the Tiger. He knew the tank contained five men along with a powerful cannon capable of firing four different types of projectiles, including armor-piercing ones. This was the very thing he needed to take out of action to let the Allies' reinforcements arrive. With the do-or-die order, no one was going anywhere, so it was up to him to turn the tide as best he could.

He opened up the access port and reached inside, grabbing the startled commander's hat. As the blond man stared up, a red-gloved fist broke his nose, staggering him into his loader. Two arms reached within and hauled the man out of the tank and then over the side in one smooth, continuous motion. Cap wedged his shield into place on the exterior and dropped into the commander's now-vacant position. Swiftly, he cracked the loader's head against the steel side and reached forward to grab the gunner, who was reaching for his sidearm. Instead, he found his hand enveloped in the red-gloved vise that caused bones to pop. A left hook staggered him, and Cap grabbed the man's head and rammed it into the driver's.

A few more body blows left neither man capable of fighting back, and Cap reached between them and shut down the engine. He wished he had the time to move them and gain control of the weaponry, but stopping the tank would do.

As he emerged topside and retrieved his shield, more

tanks, mortars and antitank guns filled his field of vision. Even if he didn't have to fend off enemy fire, Cap didn't have the time or strength to take them all on. Instead, he had to make a statement—something big, something to rally the Allies who, at the moment, were outgunned by whatever that new weapon was. And that new weapon was intelligence he needed for himself, and to make certain Command knew of its existence.

Seeing that an antitank gun nearby was being turned and aimed at the very tank he was standing on, he bent his knees, made a quick mental calculation, and sprang up. He somersaulted in the air and landed atop a cluster of soldiers, ducking gunfire along the way. With his shield upraised, he avoided a hail of fresh gunfire, then tossed the shield forward, taking out the men manning the antitank mortar with surprising ease. Cordite, gunpowder, and blood added foul odors to the desert air, and he noted the temperature was dropping while the fighting heated up.

Cap could tell more than one turret was being aimed his way, and he didn't have much time. As it was, more German soldiers were advancing into view, none seemingly worried about friendly fire. The mortar was loaded, so he needed to take careful aim, fire, and then get the hell of out of there. He just needed a target, and spotted what appeared to be fuel trucks and ammunition stacked near one another—out of the way, or so it seemed.

This looked like a Pak 36, firing 37 mm shells, and accurate to approximately 3,300 feet. He estimated the distance to the fuel truck to be closer to 2,000 feet, so he adjusted the sight a few times, then fired. Fierce kickback staggered him briefly, but then seconds later came the sound of impact and explosions. The night sky turned fiery orange then yellow and red as the truck burst apart, its heat setting off some of the stacked ammunition.

Using the detonation as cover, he rushed through a gang of soldiers, his shield brushing them to either side, and then he was racing back to the Allies. Shots rang out, and two managed to hit the chain mail, causing him to stumble, but Cap never faltered until he reached cover behind a British tank.

"Captain Bloody America," the man beside him said in amazement.

"You okay, Yank?" another asked. "Looked to me like you were shot."

Cap rolled over to let the man inspect his right shoulder blade and suddenly felt very tired. When he righted himself, the English private said, "Dents, no blood."

"Thanks."

The first soldier handed him a canteen, which he thirstily drained. "What's the situation?"

"We're holding them off for now, and whatever you destroyed can only help," the man said.

"They're firing something new, powerful," Cap noted.

"It's some blasted six-barreled rocket mortar, never seen the like before," he was told. "Wicked effective. It's how they broke through the first line of defense."

"Rommel's been winning this round," the weary American soldier said.

"He may have won the first round, but this fight's far from over. Buck up, man."

"I need to report back to Command," Captain America said, slowly rising to a crouch. "Which way?"

"American commanders are that way, I think," the second man said, pointing.

Later, Cap would learn more than a thousand men died in that first round, and many more before the Allies prevailed, bloodying Rommel's nose. It was, at the time, America's most serious defeat and largest loss of life. There might have been more losses had Captain America not been present. The outcome of the battle sank in that the war was not going to end quickly, and that countless more men would die before then. And while he could fight each day, the numbers were against him—while one man can make a difference, he would have to choose his time and place. That night, his presence helped, but with him in Africa, who was not getting his help in England or France or Belgium? The enormity of the fighting weighed on him.

CHAPTER TWO

The motorcade from the airport consisted of seven heavily armored SUVs. Within one of the vehicles, the two congressional aides gawked through the windows. Lining the streets of Slorenia were protestors, many anti-American, many anti-Slorene—all equally loud. The cloudy day cast a grayness on everything, which matched the war-torn buildings, chunks of construction and rubble scattered everywhere one looked. What few people who could be spied beyond the protestors were in dingy clothing, many begging, a few selling fruits and vegetables from baskets at their feet.

". . . we have the luncheon, then the meeting with the trade delegation," Martinez was saying, recounting the itinerary. He had already been nicknamed "the official timekeeper" by the other congressmen.

"It's one thing to read a report and watch a video," Gabby Lewin said, interrupting the recitation. "This is something else entirely. It's just so . . ."

". . . sad," finished Gallo.

"Another example of religious fanaticism," Martinez said in his soft voice.

"They would rather exterminate one another than come together to rebuild," Seaver added, a twang in his voice.

"If that's true, which I doubt," Captain America said, "why are we here?"

"The one thing going for them is their drone manufacturing. Hereward Corp. swooped in after that Ultron mess and put a large number of people to work. They've since gained a certain expertise that we'd like to see put to work for us," he said. "I have empty factories in my state I could be filling with workers."

"You were there, right?" Gallo, seated beside the hero, asked.

"Yes, it was one of the bloodiest battles I've ever been in," he said in a quiet tone. He'd been in plenty of battles across the years. As Steve Rogers, his eyes were opened when they first hit the African shores, and again when America got its first taste of defeat against the Axis. Loss and sacrifice were a part of every soldier's life, he knew, but here the countless innocent lives lost staggered his imagination.

Cap fell silent, not wishing to discuss the incident, but his mind couldn't help but flash back to those terrible days just a few years previous. He and his fellow Avengers had had to fight the eighteenth iteration of Ultron, the android created by fellow Avenger Hank Pym, and this one had a body made of pure Adamantium. Ultron replicated his earlier selves and duplicated massive numbers, laying waste to most of Slorenia before the Avengers could stop him. By then, though, thousands had been killed, including the country's protectors: the Black Brigade and Ember. The latter was the country's mystic champion, a balancing force against the evil Volkhy, who lived underground and secretly controlled the governing council of Slorenia. Since Ultron's defeat, the country seemed bereft of its supernatural forces—a temporary situation at best, he knew. Thankfully, he wouldn't have to deal with magic this trip.

If Goliath hadn't used Vibranium to shatter Ultron, Cap wondered if there would have been another way to stop the construct. As it was, the souls of the dead had wound up trapped in the Ebony Blade, now in the possession of poor Sean Dolan, who had been transformed into the being called Bloodwraith. Thanks to Wanda Maximoff, Dolan was mystically tied to Slorenian soil, unable to hurt others. From last reports, he had retreated deep within the interior of the small country and left the survivors alone, letting them begin the long process of rebuilding and healing.

Given how much history had soaked into the land, Captain America was filled with memories, and silently hoped he would not be creating any additional negative experiences; the country had seen enough of that over the centuries.

The caravan slowly traveled from the airport into

Tblunka, the capital city. In the distance, Rogers could see evidence of construction equipment, stark against the dark clouds. If it was in his power to help, when he had failed so many previously, he would do his part—even if it meant more handshakes, hugs, and selfies.

"Their success has made them of interest to the Russians," Martinez continued, breaking Cap from his dark thoughts.

"They're behind on unmanned aerial vehicle tech, and that would fill a gap they have," the congressman added. "I'd rather we strike a deal with them so we can protect their interests, and our own."

"What are they so angry about? What have we done to them?"

"Gabby, think about it. Who built Ultron? An Avenger. An American," Gallo said.

"It's more than that," Martinez interrupted. "The religious divide between the Dudak and Slorene people is generations old, and the tensions resurfaced—again—*after* Ultron. Yes, there's some anger directed at America for not stepping up and sending them billions, but we're just an excuse for their anger."

"I see someone has been brushing up on his briefing books," Seaver said, a broad grin on his face.

"One of us needed to be the expert. It also allowed me an understanding to help craft the ideal itinerary," Martinez replied.

"You've really softened your stand on the order of countries," Lewin said. "Two months ago, you insisted on Slorenia first."

"I was overruled," Martinez said, nodding his head in Ojeda's direction.

The city was a mix of architectural styles that showed changing tastes and evolving materials. Many shops were still boarded up, and some buildings half standing. But there were signs of life, with new construction and people safely walking the streets in comparison with the poverty Cap had spotted elsewhere. Somewhere beyond the city limits was a Stark factory, and he wondered whether it still stood; he suspected a visit from the Golden Avenger would quickly follow if there was trouble, which could well turn things into a diplomatic incident.

The SUVs wended their way through narrow, winding streets until they came to a stop at an impressive fortress-like stone building where the Tabissara, the ten elected leaders, managed the government. Cap knew they were also hiring mercenaries to help put down protests, pitting their interests against Hereward, disliking the presence of a foreign investor. While he longed for simpler times, he also recognized that "his" time was equally complex, although the divisions between right and wrong were far clearer.

The local police, in black and red uniforms—some carrying rifles, others machine pistols—stood at attention while junior aides simultaneously opened the doors on the seven vehicles. Everyone stood on the street, taking in the sight. Cap scanned the vicinity, searching for trouble, but he saw nothing alarming, and the protestors' noise was dim in the background. Clearly, they'd been kept away from this building, where the talks were to be held. Each delegate stretched while Gallo and some of the press snapped pictures.

Amberson walked over to Captain America and, to make it clear this was an off-the-record conversation, showed his recorder was in his pocket. "How's it feel to be back?"

"Sad," Cap said, hands behind his back. "They didn't ask for Ultron's attack. They didn't deserve it, and it looks like things are only marginally better."

"The religious divide wasn't so obvious back then," Amberson said. "I consider myself lucky to have gotten out alive. I'd be lying if I said I didn't have the odd nightmare about Ultron-whatever making a return appearance."

He gestured to the northwest corner, away from the main building. "I was right there, doing a stand-up for the evening news when you rushed by and told me to get away. Seconds later, half a building came tumbling down. I ran, but I also saw at least a dozen crushed under all that."

Cap placed a comforting hand on the reporter's shoulder and said, "That's war, Aaron. The people survived, and we're here to do something positive."

"Just getting them to talk would be good for starters,"

Amberson said. "I hear things have been stirred up to new heights."

"You've got strong sources to tap into for your coverage. Use them. I have to go in with the others. See you at the press conference."

Captain America walked over to the delegation, and they were escorted into the building. Without much fanfare, the group was taken to a large conference room. Several tables were set, each with name placards to identify places. Along one wall were coffee urns and the ubiquitous mountain of plastic water bottles. There was no sign of food, which he knew would elicit grumblings from the ever-hungry Gallo. As the Americans found their places, a door at the rear of the mammoth, high-ceilinged room opened, and the ten members of the Tabissara entered. Behind them came a flurry of aides and, finally, three people representing Hereward. They were clearly from the Swedish home offices, judging by the paler complexions and uniform blond hair. The women were in business dresses, complete with shawls to fight the heavy air conditioning; the sole man was in a dark-navy suit that spoke of his salary.

There was little fuss and minimal introductions, as the Tabissara wanted to get right to work on the negotiations. Any chitchat, they felt, could be saved for the dinner following the press conference—one, Cap noted, they had been reluctant to allow but had been forced into by the

Americans. Rogers' seat was at a rear table, beside Gallo and Lewin, where it was clear he was not expected to participate. Glancing down, he looked at the printed agenda, which was in both English and Slovak. Tomorrow's schedule included a brief tour of the city and surrounding countryside—an opportunity for the Slorenian people to see their government in action, and of course, to show off their one-time savior.

Meetings like this were beyond his interests, especially when he had little to contribute. He'd have preferred walking the city, but he was discouraged from doing so by the Tabissara's primary statesman, Juris Bosholov. Idly, Rogers wondered how the Tabissara functioned without Volkhvy's malevolent influence. The briefing Rogers had been given indicated all ten other members were of the majority people, and their policies definitely discriminated against the Dudak. It all had something to do with ancient religious beliefs, prejudices now made into laws. He asked himself, for far from the first time, when people would learn to coexist without letting their differences be used as wedges.

Lewin and Gallo, casual and friendly in private, were incredibly efficient and professional when at work, he noticed. Each was taking notes, comparing information with their briefings and shared summaries. Both ignored their tablets and phones, likely for fear of being tapped, given the rampant paranoia they sensed from the government, and they didn't let the mind-numbing discussion of trade balances lull them to sleep.

For his part, Cap used the time to step away from the others and sort his thoughts about the mission, Scattershot, and the possibilities her attack presented. Certain he was alone, Cap opened a secure comm link with the S.H.I.E.L.D. Helicarrier *Crescent* and spoke with the head of their security detail, a broad-shouldered, olive-skinned agent named Ohlmert. "Yes, sir, Scattershot is securely in custody. Our dampeners have her powers curtailed," he said in a deep voice.

His clipped words indicated his rigorous training and respect for the chain of command; Captain America enjoyed not only his Avengers status, but also had a special place in S.H.I.E.L.D.'s hierarchy.

"Any luck with the interrogation?"

"I wish I had something positive to report, Captain," Ohlmert said. "Since you gave her to us yesterday, she's been tighter than a clam."

"In other words, not a peep."

"I'd take a peep—at least that would be a sound. She's been mute, not even a 'thank you' when she's been fed."

"Have you managed to track her whereabouts before the attack?"

"Again, I wish I had something substantive to share, sir, but we're continuing to do fieldwork to determine her previous twenty-four to forty-eight hours."

Rogers was frustrated with the lack of intelligence when there were so many questions to answer, but that certainly wasn't Ohlmert's fault.

The Symkarian king was still mulling over whether to charge Scattershot with crimes and bring her back to Symkaria for trial or turn her over to the International Criminal Court for war crimes. Symkaria's envoy to Russia had also reported back that the Kremlin had disavowed Scattershot, which could well be the case. Still, she didn't attack for no reason at all, and that gnawed at Rogers.

His attention was drawn back to the meeting when Bosholov, a corpulent man with an aggressive demeanor, slapped his hand hard on his conference table and shouted something in his native tongue about wood exports. The Americans, wearing earbud translators, winced at what he said, something about being taken advantage of. The Slorenian's eyes flared, and his face was red with anger, evidence of something above and beyond a simple misunderstanding. Suddenly, he rose and marched out of the room, leaving everyone temporarily speechless.

"What was that all about?" Cap asked Lewin.

She shrugged. "I can't figure out what set him off like that. Martinez asked about a trade imbalance from last year." They settled back as one of the members spoke as if his colleague was never there.

The tedious afternoon dragged on until finally the

meeting adjourned. Cap was fairly certain something got settled, but he was unsure of exactly what. Bosholov had not returned, nor was his absence commented on by the Tabissara. With the talks over, a team of government men and women arrived to escort the delegation to the adjacent hotel, where they could freshen up before the dinner.

They crossed the street, enjoying the cooling early evening. The protestors were close now, shouting more at one another than at the Americans. Rogers couldn't make out what was being said beyond the heated tones, so he asked their translator, a pretty young college student for help.

"One side is arguing the Dudak were invaders, taking the Slorenes' land and jobs."

"Is that true?" he asked her.

"Maybe, when the Dudak first arrived, but certainly not now."

"When did they arrive?"

"About six thousand years ago," she said, looking directly at Cap, waiting for his reaction.

"You're kidding me," he said, surprised.

"I wish I were. In time, the Slorenes drove the Dudak off their farms, aided by their god, Ember. So the Dudak invoked their god, Volkvhy. The unrest isolated the country while trade elsewhere in Europe flourished. Then resentment built up over that, too."

"This sounds terrible," Seaver said. "And frankly, not too dissimilar to strife in other countries."

"And childish," Jackson added.

"So much effort wasted on prolonging misery," Martinez quietly added.

Cap wondered whether the protestors would keep it up all night. Such sustained passion was not a good sign, and no doubt was impeding the country's ability to recover and thrive after Ultron's devastation.

* * *

The air was cooler than the day before as Captain America and two of the delegates walked together as part of the tour. They had been split into three groups, taking different routes that assured everyone would see everything, but keeping the parties more manageable. Members of the press were equally divided, and he was glad to have Amberson on his team—less so the assertive Singer, who continued to pepper the delegates with questions, even directing a few at him.

What captured Rogers' notice was that Bosholov was calmer today, almost as if yesterday's outburst never happened. At the dinner the previous night, he was all apologies and made many toasts throughout the proceedings. He put away a fair amount of alcohol, but today didn't seem any worse for the indulgence.

They were at a park that served as both nature preserve and war memorial. Slorenia had been a part of the USSR, another land grab Joseph Stalin made in the waning days of the Second World War. Today, the country was independent, but Russia's shadow loomed large. Several portions of the land were still cratered where missiles had fallen during the war, and were now roped off and preserved as a reminder of war's horrors. The sight brought back many memories to the Avenger.

"You see off to the right, those low hills?" Cap asked Amberson.

"Sure."

"We stopped two tanks from rolling over a pinned-down squad," Cap recalled. "Allied Command had dispatched us here to lend support before reinforcements could arrive. The Nazis were crossing through Slorenia to get at the Russian flank."

"How do you remember each battle so clearly?"

"War has a way of indelibly etching itself in your mind, I suppose. I may not recall every name or how we fought each battle, but I can picture where we were, when we fought . . ." He trailed off.

"And by we, you mean you and Bucky."

The soldier just nodded, letting his mind flash back to the attack. How they dropped from their tree cover and overwhelmed the lead tank. How, as he fought atop the tank, Bucky managed to get below, take out the driver, and swivel the turret to fire on the tank behind. In fairly short order, four German tanks were out of action, and the American and British squadron was able to recover and move forward.

The remainder of the tour was fairly quiet as Cap reminisced to himself while Congressman Jackson and Congresswoman Ojeda talked with Bosholov and the press. As they neared the park's entrance, though, their cars were blocked by a fresh wave of Dudak protestors insisting on a place among the Tabissara, an end to their persecution, and more jobs. The Slorenian police, seemingly unprepared for the protest, were outnumbered and ill equipped. Slipping out of the car opposite the crowd, Cap removed the shield from his back, gripped it tight, and studied the scene, exploring scenarios that would calm things down the fastest and inflict the least harm.

To his credit, Bosholov waded past his guards and stood directly before the crowd. He patted the air before him, encouraging the protestors to quiet down so he could speak. When the din lowered, his face contorted to absolute fury, and he yelled, "You do not deserve a seat! You should be lucky we let you serve us!"

Not at all what the Star-Spangled Avenger had expected to hear.

Bosholov was acting as he had the day before. Was he always this volatile? On some medication that had stopped working?

Cap's thoughts were interrupted, not only by a fresh wave of disapproval, but by a second angry crowd, this one made up of the Slorene majority. This group didn't have placards, instead gripped chains, sticks, and even tire irons. Things were about to get ugly, fast. He was striding forth to quell the situation when Ojeda reached out and grabbed his thick bicep.

"It's an internal matter," she said.

"There's going to be bloodshed. They've lost enough," he protested.

"You enter the fight, that becomes the news, and their message vanishes."

"And when Swanson or Singer shoots B-roll of me on the sidelines, what's the story then? I *cannot* stand aside in the name of politics," he said through gritted teeth.

"You're no better than your ancestors, ready to roll over and hand over our land to the Russians, like they did in the First World War!" Bosholov yelled at the Slorene faction. Then he spun about and addressed the Dudak side. "And your ancestors made peace with their enemies, so how dare you try and divide us!"

To Cap, the messages as translated for him by Ojeda sounded inconsistent, but what was clear was that Bosholov was doing little to mollify either side.

While the words were foreign, the tone from all sides was hostile and getting louder. Any second now, by intent or accident, weapons would be used and then people would be hurt. He remained baffled about simmering tensions lasting six thousand years, but that was a discussion for another time.

Captain America was convinced something was very wrong.

"Lewin! Gallo!" he commanded. They tore their attention away from the brewing fight and hurried over. "Keep your eyes sharp—I think we have an agitator in the area. Someone's manipulating them all," he explained.

Then, as if he was following Ojeda's instructions, Cap stepped backward until he was behind the tour group. Away from the verbal distractions, he scanned the area slowly, a few degrees at a time. There were birds, squirrels, a stray dog—but no other people. Everything was natural, including the trees, bushes, and flower beds. The partly cloudy sky didn't offer a hint of an aerial option. He was nearly done with his scan when something flickered to his left, in his peripheral vision. Cap pretended to keep scanning to create the illusion he wasn't suddenly tense from head to toe. His focus remained on the spot behind a cluster of trees and bushes, and he was rewarded with a clear sight of steel toes. They were oversized for a human, more like a wolf's clawed paws.

That was most certainly not a part of the park.

Why would someone in steel plating or armor want to remain hidden, and how could they be causing the protest to morph into a riot? The rise and fall of the yelling, nearly matching the pendulum-like swings of Bosholov's mood, was not what anyone would call normal behavior. Long experience with the likes of manipulators like Doctor Faustus and other telepathically gifted foes told him there was emotional or mental manipulation going on. And once he clicked on to that, his analytic mind called up the other members of Peristrike Force. Following the earlier attack, he had refreshed his memory of them—including their oldest member, Nikolai Vonya, the cyborg called Psi-Wolf.

Cap recalled that the S.H.I.E.L.D. dossier said that Psi-Wolf's brother, Professor Anatoly Vonya, was the mad genius behind the Soviet super human–powers program. Something had gone wrong with Nikolai's procedure, which resulted in the need for biomechanical grafts that provided him with bionic arms, legs, and eyes, along with a large sonic gun on his right arm and an oversized gun at his shoulder. The newly made Nikolai stood seven feet tall and was nicknamed the "Dreaded One" for his passionate zeal to restore Russia to its former glory. As a result, Nikolai considered himself an agent of change, not a terrorist. His natural telepathic gifts were enhanced substantially by the helmet he wore. From what Cap could recall, Psi-Wolf was limited to influencing one mind at a time, which might explain how Bosholov was at times rational and at times not. By picking citizens on both sides of the cultural divide, Vonya was able to incite the riot now unfolding.

That made things simpler for the Avenger. If Ojeda didn't want him mixing it up with the citizens, he would just have to go after Psi-Wolf. That shouldn't trouble her, as Cap wouldn't be interfering with the country's sovereignty. It was just a matter of gaining the upper hand on Vonya without getting his own mind trapped. Once more, he surveyed the area and realized his red, white, and blue uniform removed subtlety as an option. Instead, he'd need a more direct approach, and favored speed to keep Vonya busy.

With that, he twisted his torso, planted his feet, and adjusted his arm, then swiveled around, unleashing the shield into the air. It arced past the trees and Vonya's hiding spot, catching the bigger man's attention. This gave the Avenger time to break into a dead run, directly at him.

The shield arced and began its return flight. Vonya took aim with his shoulder-mounted gun. A single shot rang out as a dark projectile intercepted the shield, without doing damage to anything but its momentum. As Vonya turned to face Captain America, the hero was already leaping in the air to close the distance between them. His 240 pounds turned him into a force akin to a cannonball, and he slammed into Vonya's armored body. The two men toppled to the ground, the heavier Russian digging deep ruts in the grass.

His fists useless against the armor, Captain America focused on the man's white-bearded face. He managed one punch before the larger man rolled onto his side and tossed his attacker to the ground. The sonic weapon had been charging and now dispensed a shot at Captain America, landing a solid blow to his back. The chain mail absorbed and dispersed most of the force, but the sheer impact left him momentarily stunned. Psi-Wolf took advantage of the moment, rising to his feet and stomping down hard on Cap's left shoulder blade with a crunching sound. Nothing broke, but it hurt like hell.

Scrambling to his feet, Captain America confronted the Russian zealot.

"Why are you doing this?"

"For the glory of Russia!" He sounded like a fanatic, and Cap had heard it all before. In fact, there was something tiresome about Psi-Wolf in his overly armored, heavily weaponed form, his brother's compensation for the injuries the experiments caused. There had to be more to his reason, and being the second member of Peristrike Force to commit such as act set off mental alarms in Cap's mind. Any consideration would have to wait, because if Psi-Wolf tried, he could capture Cap's will.

It was time to take him down.

Cap charged at him once more and leapt into the air, eluding the armored arms, and pushed off the man's shoulders, sailing over his head. Smoothly, he landed on the grass and scooped up his shield, putting it between him and Psi-Wolf. Charging once more, he launched himself at his opponent and used the shield as a battering ram, knocking the unwieldy figure over. Despite the heavy weight of the Russian's armor, Cap flipped over him, landed on his feet, pivoted, and hurled the shield. The disc sailed with unerring aim, dislodging the shoulder gun with a tearing sound of metal.

Psi-Wolf cursed in Russian and aimed once more with the sonic gun on his right arm. It was going to be a race between the sonic blast and the shield returning to its owner.

Cap gritted his teeth for the impact, knowing full well the speed of sound would win. The shield, though, was caught in the beam, making the blast ineffective.

Seizing the opportunity, he charged at Vonya, letting himself get caught in the massive, metallic arms while keeping his own free. Psi-Wolf squeezed, and Cap could feel his ribs begin to ache and maybe crack under the super-human pressure. He just had to endure it long enough to reach behind Vonya. With his own enhanced strength, he tore away the remains of the gun mounting on the shoulder and dug into the armor, grasping at wiring. Ragged metal tore at his leather gloves, but he kept digging. His fingers felt wires and traced them to distribution nodes. Grasping a handful, he yanked as he let out a cry of pain.

Psi-Wolf tried to tighten his grip, but it proved futile as Cap moved to reach deeper. Still, the pressure on his ribs was enormous, and he feared the chain mail would not hold out for much longer.

Once a few wires tore free, he reached deeper and pulled out anything he could, figuring the more damage the better. There was a sizzling sound, then tortured mechanical clicks. He had done enough damage to cause a cascading electronic failure that seemed to immobilize the armor.

"I have you now," Vonya snarled.

Cap felt something tug at his mind, but he fought against it as he unsteadily wriggled from the cyborg's frozen grip. He'd dealt with telepaths of all power levels, and had studied with several to erect mental barriers that, if not perfect, provided an unusual level of protection for a mortal. Crouching before the Russian, he felt the mother of all headaches and knew he had seconds before those barriers collapsed. Using this time, he cocked back a fist and pummeled Vonya's face, breaking his nose and stunning the man. As blood turned the snow-white beard crimson, Cap, gasping, reached with both hands to pry loose the enhancing helmet, leaving the man severely restricted both physically and mentally. Psi-Wolf was still a natural telepath, but Cap knew distance would blunt any influence he could muster, especially injured and in pain as he was. Still, the man had to remain unconscious until the right equipment could be summoned.

Sweat dripping down the inside of his uniform, aching all over, and nursing at least one cracked rib, Cap shakily stood up. He retrieved his shield and backed away from the groaning Russian. Behind him, he could hear the rioters and the sounds of running feet closing in. Cap dared a glance over a shoulder to see Lewin and several police officers charging his way.

"Don't shoot! He's down," Cap yelled. He hoped the tone would transcend the language barrier.

When Lewin, huffing, joined them, he held out his gloved hand. "Your transceiver, please."

She cocked her head, but complied. He took the earbud and handed it to a policeman, pantomiming that he should wear it. The man looked dubious, but standing before an Avenger led him to the only possible conclusion: he put it in his ear as Lewin said, "Ewww."

"Do you understand me?"

The policeman, in his forties with a thick brown mustache that matched his eyebrows, widened his eyes and nodded.

"This man remains dangerous. I've immobilized his armor, but he can still influence your mind. Keep your distance, but keep him guarded until help arrives so he can be properly secured."

"Of course, Captain."

"Good man."

Aching, his uniform singed and ragged in spots, Cap surveyed the damage. It was clear that the people were no longer being inflamed by Psi-Wolf. He saw pockets of people crying and hugging one another, ashamed of their words and deeds. Some had been injured and were now caring for one another. Others were staring into space, completely baffled by what had happened to them. The air was filled with new sounds instead of shouting. There was weeping, some laughs, and a murmur. Deeper in the background were the sirens of police and ambulances rushing to the scene. Police on hand were assisting those in the most distress, and were being helped by the former protestors. The innate distrust between sides was so easy to inflame, but there was little he could do about it during so brief a visit. At least he was able to stop the immediate bloodshed. The rest was up to them.

Slowly, he walked back to the rattled Americans and their host, Bosholov, who, despite his usually gruff demeanor, looked genuinely relieved to see him. Through the interpreter, he asked, "What has happened?"

"No one could be that passionate about wood exports," Cap said. "You have been mentally manipulated, exacerbating any resentment you have toward the delegation. Today, that was expanded to incite this near riot."

"You're serious, aren't you?"

"To you, this may seem a fantastic thing, but to me, it's a Thursday," the American said with a reassuring grin.

"If what you say is true, the rioters actually harbor these feelings toward one another?"

"It seems that way," Cap said. "I find it astounding anyone can hold a six-thousand-year old grudge."

Bosholov grunted with a tight smile. "The old ways wax and wane like the moon. I see we have more work ahead of us."

"Who the hell was that?" asked Seaver as the Slorenian minister wandered off to speak with some of the protestors, a policeman accompanying him for safety.

"His name is Psi-Wolf, and he comes from the same team as Scattershot," Rogers told them.

"So, the Russians are behind this?" Lewin asked.

"That's jumping to a conclusion, Gabby. They may be Russian, but they are not the country's official super-team."

"Two countries and two attacks is no coincidence," she said.

"I will agree on that. And whereas Scattershot was all about physical destruction, this was far more invasive, with longer-lasting repercussions," Cap said.

"I am disgusted he used my own peoples' prejudices for his personal gain," Bosholov said as he returned to the group, prompting the press to rush past Gallo, who had tried to keep them at bay.

"How close to the surface are those tensions?" Swanson began, while Singer wanted to get Bosholov on the record about security measures. She was clearly looking to show how unprepared the country was. Ojeda gamely stepped up to diffuse that line of questioning.

And so it went, with Captain America letting the Americans and their Slorenian host deal with the questions. He was tired and wanted some privacy to check—and most likely tape—his ribs. Not for the first time, he was counting on the advanced healing properties of the super-soldier serum to get him ready for the next attack, because now he was certain there would be one.

At an opportune moment, he caught Congresswoman Ojeda's eye, and she walked over. She glanced at his battered uniform and the look in his eyes. "Are you okay, Captain?"

"I will be, but I need a secure communications facility and some first-aid supplies. Nothing for the press to know about."

"Of course. Should we find a doctor?"

"I can handle it myself, thanks," Cap said, knowing he should have a doctor check him out, but not wanting to give away how sore and battered he felt.

"I'm worried," Ojeda said. "Maybe we should cut the itinerary short."

"I wouldn't do that."

"Martinez would certainly complain about all his work going up in smoke," she mused, a twinkle in her eye despite the grim situation.

"I know I'm supposed to be just a symbol on this trip, but I'm the best security you have. As good as the army and police might be, they are no match for the likes of Peristrike Force."

"How many more are there?"

"Beyond these two, Siberion and Volga Belle," he said.

Ojeda frowned at the names, trying to recall them, then shook her head. "Have you fought them before? Can you stop them?"

"No, I've only scanned their records. They're not terribly active, according to S.H.I.E.L.D. intelligence. Siberion and Volga Belle were seen in Vladivostok just last week. It's why I don't think they're here on behalf of the Russian government."

"How does that follow?" Ojeda asked.

"If there were two attacks and we have more countries to visit, then more attacks may be expected. If Peristrike Force were contracted, they'd already be on their way."

Ojeda nodded, clearly not entirely convinced.

She frowned at that. "Who then?"

"I don't know, but we need to find out, which is why I think it's best if we keep to the plan. I can always call in reinforcements if need be."

Ojeda studied Cap's face and flicked her eyes down at his marred, dirty chain mail. Thoughtful for another moment, she finally nodded once. "I have a secure satellite phone in our transportation; it should let you make your call."

"Thanks."

With that, he ignored the media questions yelled in his direction and walked gingerly to the car where the phone was. He dialed a number, let it ring once, then hung up. Within seconds, the phone rang again, the caller ID reading "Barbershop."

"Sharon?"

"Hi, Steve. Are you okay? Are the congressmen safe?"

"Yes and yes." Tersely, he filled her in, explained his most immediate need to keep Psi-Wolf inactive, and then asked for more detailed intelligence on Peristrike Force. Once done, she confirmed the orders.

"Do you want me to come?"

"Where are you now?"

"My Helicarrier is crossing Pennsylvania, but I could hop on a transport and be in Europe in a few hours."

"Thanks, but I think I have this for now. Could the *Crescent* shadow us for now since we might need more help? Who's in charge over there?"

"That'd be Captain Farrell Phillips."

"Good man," Cap said, recalling meeting the commander of the *Crescent* shortly after being introduced to the global intelligence and defense agency. He was a former pilot and could be counted on during tense situations.

"We're talking with the International Criminal Court about Scattershot, since Symkaria doesn't want her back on their soil," she said.

"I'm sure King Stefan will be pleased to hear that," Cap said, longing to be having this conversation in person. The price of duty was constantly keeping the two apart—and when they did have time to talk, it was all business. "Any word on where she was prior to the attack?"

"Not yet, and we're running her financials as best we can. You'd be surprised at how sophisticated Russian cyber-security has gotten."

"And we still have eyes on Siberion and Volga Belle?"

"One is on a date, the other at a casino in Monte Carlo."

"Okay, then they're not a current threat."

"I agree."

"But, Steve, there are two more cities . . ."

". . . and maybe two more attacks."

"Maybe? Do you need backup?"

"I've got this," he assured her. "Sharon, I've got to go."

"Miss you."

"Me too."

As he closed the secure connection, the rest of the Americans were returning to their cars. Glancing up, he could already see the Helicarrier's silhouette in the distance. Psi-Wolf would be contained, and Rogers could focus on the delegation until there was time to study his next prospective opponents in greater detail. Everyone was silent on their way back to the hotel, which was now surrounded by the small country's tiny army, complete with tanks at all four corners.

"Overkill," Martinez muttered.

"I feel safer," Gallo said, trying to lighten the mood.

"I don't," Ojeda added. "Psi-Wolf could easily have any one of them fire on the others or somehow get all four to fire on the hotel."

"Do you want to leave, Roberta?"

"No. We have our itinerary to keep, right, Pedro? And Americans do not shy away from a fight—right, Captain?"

"We fight when it's unavoidable," he told the group.

* * *

Hours later, his ribs taped and cuts cleaned by a doctor sent by the government despite his insistence otherwise, Steve Rogers toweled himself off in his small hotel room. His helmet circuitry had already confirmed it was bug free, so he could sit with a S.H.I.E.L.D.-issued tablet and fresh pot of coffee. The reports on Peristrike Force were comprehensive, but brief. They'd fought the one-time armored hero Darkhawk and seemingly vanished from active work. For them to reappear now was odd. There was a hidden hand manipulating events, but he would be damned if he could figure out who or why.

The Tabissara and the delegates were to have a quiet dinner instead of the more formal affair that had originally been planned. A separate meal and locale was arranged for the press. Last he saw, Gallo was searching for a good Wi-Fi signal, and Lewin was making them both plates for a private dinner. Cap hoped he could be more productive without outside interference or the need to preen for the media.

Sipping the bitter coffee, he considered, as Nick Fury had taught him long ago, who would benefit from an attack on Symkaria and Slorenia. Both were small Eastern European countries with meager economies, as were Carnelia and Transia, the other stops to come. Carnelia and Transia had no such forces active, so they were even more exposed.

No obvious answers were coming to mind, although he could sense the beginning of a rare headache. Thumbing off the tablet, Cap sat back, closed his eyes, and hoped for a better tomorrow.

When Captain America heard that King Victor Emmanuel III had surrendered to the Allied forces three days earlier, he thought things would begin to wrap up, that he might even be home by Christmas. Instead, he was ordered to Rome when Hitler initiated Operation Axis, a German takeover of Italy. As Nazi troops poured into the city, it was his duty to escort General Badoglio and the royal family to the south, where they intended to establish an antifascist government. A British transport had rushed him from Dover to Italy.

On the flight, Cap opened a sealed envelope handed to him just before he boarded. Within was intelligence from the OSS that suggested Master Man was being dispatched as part of the operation and was likely going after the seventy-four-year old king and his family, to crush any hope of rebellion. There was word Hitler wanted the king arrested by Master Man, who was responsible for that assignment. That made Cap ruefully chuckle since his German counterpart appeared to have as many lives as a cat. They had first encountered one another when Baron Strucker used Master Man and a coterie of super-powered agents to invade the secretive African nation of Wakanda in search of their invaluable Vibranium ore. During the battle, the country's king, in his guise as Black Panther, injected a deadly toxin into not only Master Man, but also Warrior Woman. And yet, weeks later, there were reports both had somehow survived.

Master Man had also apparently fallen to his death in the first battle between the super-powered Invaders and the Axis super-powered agents. And was seen again not long after.

Just as he had failed in killing Winston Churchill, Master Man would have to lose once more.

This changed how Captain America would have to operate, shifting from covert surveillance and protection as Victor Emmanuel and his wife, Elena, left Rome. Now, he'd have to be seen, a deterrent to Master Man and, hopefully, the Nazi army.

Radio reports indicated that once the armistice was announced, the Italian troops were aimless, awaiting orders as to what to do, whom to fight, and whom to obey. As a result, they were overwhelmed when the Nazis arrived, with many shot, others arrested and imprisoned. The chaos would prove beneficial to both Cap and Master Man, so he needed to be especially wary. Ideally, he'd have American troop support, a detached group such as the Howling Commandos or

Leatherneck Raiders—even Bucky would have been helpful, but the teen was back in England. Cap was on his own.

The plane dared to fly low over the city, allowing the American hero to parachute into the densely wooded Villa Ada park. As he leapt from the plane, just before it banked right and began to climb, not wanting to risk enemy fire, there was the familiar rush of cold air on his skin. Once he landed, Cap hid his parachute and navigated the ruined streets leading to the massive Quirinal Palace, which sprawled for blocks in every direction. Someday, he'd like to return and see the sights, which meant, of course, he'd have to ensure they were actually preserved. In the distance, he heard trucks and the occasional crack of rifle fire. No doubt, the chaos would continue for some time, but he decided he had to hurry and find a way in to where the royal family might be. His instructions were vague enough to be annoying, and the lack of a palace map would slow him down.

As he crossed Via Giovanni Giolitti, trucks carrying Italian soldiers passed by. They were still in uniform, brandishing rifles, but instead of shooting at the symbol of America, they cheered and waved at him. A week ago, they might have fired, but now they seemed genuinely happy to see him. Its suddenness surprised him, but he shook it off as he continued toward the palace, trying to avoid whichever streetlights still functioned. He noted that the sidewalks were lightly crowded, and more than a few people spotted him, the one downside to his colorful uniform. Had he worn a khaki outfit, no one would have given him a second glance. No doubt, gossip would spread that he was in the city, which would make him a sure target for the Nazis, who never seemed to sleep. Worse, it would warn Master Man.

That concern was erased when Cap heard a tremendous crunching sound, similar to a bomb detonating. The unmistakable rattle of brick and mortar tumbling down came directly from the Quirinal Palace. While most of it was two stories tall, the palace stretched endlessly and branched off, creating gardens and walkways, and there were lots of places someone as powerful as Master Man could rip open to gain access, leaving death and devastation in his wake. While the super-solider formula enhanced Cap's physical and mental skills, its German equivalent appeared to amplify Wilhelm Lohmer's arrogance in addition to granting him superior strength. There was never anything subtle about the way Master Man tackled a mission.

Shifting his approach, Captain America broke into a sprint and aimed himself at the sound of destruction. He leapt over a passing car, dodged a crowd of late-night strollers, and finally arrived in time to see Lohmer pummel a wall to dust, then jump through the newly created access point to the palace. Apparently, no one ever used the doors. Palace guards opened fire on the blue and yellow-clad blond, who proudly wore a black Swastika against a red circle on his chest. It afforded him little protection, however, given how hardened his skin had become, the bullets proved ineffective. The fusillade did annoy the easily angered German, who lifted a piece of wall and threw it down the hall at the guards. One was immediately killed on impact, while the others scattered.

Master Man didn't bother to look around as he entered the grand structure and so was completely unaware that Captain America stalked him, assessing the plaster and marble battlefield. Cap would need to choose his time wisely since the element of surprise was used just once.

Lohmer snarled as fresh guards arrived. The rapid impact of bullets ripping into his uniform did little more than anger him further. As a result, a marble sculpture of a pope became a missile, shattering a soldier's rib cage on impact. His machine gun clattered to the ground with a loud metallic crack. As others rounded a corner, they prepared to open fire and Master Man hefted more debris to use as projectiles.

Judging the distance between them, Cap rushed forward, preparing to ram his foe with the indestructible shield. His boots clacked against the marble, alerting Lohmer, who turned around, eyes widening in recognition, a wolfish grin forming on his broad face. He moved a moment too late and the full force of American might slammed into him. The smooth surface of the floor allowed Cap to shove Master Man several feet backward, and the awkward turn of his body at the moment of impact caused his foe to lose his balance. Cap took advantage of that and continued going forward, leaping over Master Man.

The German's reflexes were fast, though. As the American leapt over him, his right hand reached up, grabbed an ankle, and swung his attacker to the left, sending him into a gigantic painting. Cap slid to the ground as Master Man rose to his feet, ignoring the guards' fire as he reached down to heft his enemy into the air and send him sailing toward the guards. Bullets dented the chain mail, each impact causing Cap to grunt before he crashed to the hard floor, slid through a doorway, and stopped as he struck a brightly patterned area rug.

Rising, Cap realized he and Master Man could fight all night and reduce the world's largest palace to little more than a junkyard of antiquity. The good news was that he retained his grip on the shield, and could now use it to try to make quick work of the powerful German. With practiced ease, he flipped the shield, which sailed through the doorway and smacked into Master Man, more to cause bruising than with any hope of disabling him.

But it did draw the German's attention away from the overmatched guards. No doubt the royal family was being well protected, but if Master Man reached them, that would change in a heartbeat. The Sentinel of Liberty had to make certain the family got away safely, and that loss of life was minimized. It was a complicated equation when you added in preserving as much of the palace as possible. His opponent had always shown contempt for anything that got in his way, leaving a trail of bodies and obliteration in his wake. In those ways, each reflected their country, shrinking the Allied-Axis conflict down to these two men. If it meant an end to the war, Cap would gladly take on Master Man winner take all, but he had his doubts all countries would abide by those rules—along with the fact it would mean he would have to kill Lohmer, and taking a life was never done easily. He'd had to kill since beginning his service, but it was a challenge to minimize that at every opportunity. It had put him into conflict with many people ranging from his fellow dogfaces to Prince Namor, the vengeful son of Atlantis, whose worldview was often different from Cap's own.

Master Man turned to face Cap just as the shield returned to his reach.

"*Ich begrüsse die Chance, ihnen ein für allemal zu zeigen, dass ich das oberste Produkt der Nazi-Wissenschaft bin!*"

"I have no idea what you said, Lohmer, but I am not letting you near the king," Cap countered. Clearly, the tone was a boastful one and more than once he wished he could understand more German. He'd only learned a handful of useful words and phrases, along with quite a few colorful phrases Bucky had taught him.

Cap dashed into the first room he reached, thundering footfalls right behind him. Master Man would continue his assault on Captain America as long as possible, remaining fixated on him and not Victor Emmanuel. Master Man was aggressive and single minded, actually not all that smart or a studied tactician. Cap just needed to play Follow the Leader for a little while, hoping General Badoglio could get the royal family far away.

The room turned out to be a small sitting room of some sort, heavily decorated in a clash of styles and colors that made little sense to Cap. Then again, he was from Brooklyn, where such finery barely existed outside of magazines. There was, though, a very large window leading out to one of the gardens, and that would have to do. With his shield before him, he smashed through the glass, just eluding the German's grasp. Rolling to a stop, Cap studied his surroundings, noting that the walls were relatively smooth and high enough to make reaching the top a challenge. The space was about twenty by ninety feet, filled with the remnants of summer flowers, palm trees and greenery ringing the space along with a large, round pond containing a stone fountain with three figures.

Master Man was right behind him so the soldier turned, planted his feet and prepared to duke it out until he could form a strategy. Brawling with Master Man would be dangerous since the German's version of the formula actually made Lohman stronger and more resilient than Cap. But he also knew Lohman had had his powers drained from him and restored a year previously, and from what he could tell, was now slightly less powerful. Still, a few blows in the right place would seriously injure Cap.

They circled one another, neither man saying a word, and not just because of the language barrier. Cap let out a sigh to taunt Master Man, and pretended to check his wristwatch, affecting boredom. The German snarled, swore a German oath, and rushed. Cap was ready, legs apart, body braced. The rushing German was met with a right hook and left jab in quick order, stopping his forward momentum. Lohmer returned the assault with his own left-right combination, powerful pistons that were not easily absorbed. Cap twisted to avoid a right uppercut, delivering a stinging blow as he brought his right fist down across Lohmer's cheek. The two traded blows, blocks, and maneuvers, clouts that would have leveled even boxing champ Joe Louis.

Clearly, this would get neither man anywhere, so Cap needed to change things up. It was evident Master Man was merely an undisciplined brawler aided by his superior strength. So, Cap needed to use ingenuity. Slowly, he danced around, making Master Man move to reach him. They continued to trade punches, feints, and parries, but Lohmer seemed unaware of how far they had moved.

Cap took a punishing blow to his ribs, but it forced Master

Man to now face the pond, the gurgling of the fountain feeding it the only other sound to be heard. Cap let himself go to one knee and Master Man held off a moment rather than press his advantage. Clearly, he wanted to face the man on his feet, to defeat him standing. Cap took a breath, testing his rib cage and deeming it sound—for now. Then, he opened one gloved hand and beckoned Lohmer toward him.

Master Man accepted the invitation, his upper lip curling into a sneer, propelling himself at Cap, who didn't try to block the move, but instead grabbed the figure, twisted, and sent the German into the shallow pond. He then pounced, landing on the crumpled form and sent a withering barrage of blows to the man's softer sections, from neck to kidneys, never the same place twice, keeping the spluttering Lohmer off balance.

He backed off a moment, then reached down and hefted Master Man from the water, up and over his head before rushing through the water, building up as much momentum as the pond allowed, and ramming Master Man's back into the heavy stone statuary in the center of the pond. He heard Lohmer exhale, the wind knocked out of him, so, without letting go, rammed him a second time. And a third.

Cap dropped the stunned figure into the water, reached around from behind, and held him in place. He applied a wrestling move designed to limit airflow and after about forty seconds, Lohmer slumped, unconscious. Cap draped him against the now-cracked statues and dashed for the palace.

A small coterie of guards had arrived and watched, none daring to shoot during the fight. Without knowing Italian he hoped to communicate with the men, starting with finding the king. As soon as he said the names Victor Emmanuel and Badoglio, several bobbed their heads in understanding and gestured for him to follow. Cap pantomimed tying up Master Man and quickly—he'd prefer they used heavy chains, but he didn't know the words and had to hurry. He had no way of knowing how long the battered German would stay down. One man in particular understood and gave orders, sending two men at a run. He then saluted the American, which Cap returned and then followed his guides.

As it turned out, Victor Emmanuel and his wife, the princess, were hidden in a secret chamber. When the bald, older Badoglio saw who was knocking, he was surprised. Thankfully, he spoke some English, as did the king. It was clear the time had come to leave, and they hurried from the palace.

While hiding them in the back of a farm truck, Cap wondered how long his counterpart would remain out of action and if there would there be fresh complications before they could reach the chosen destination of Pescara in the south.

No doubt he and Master Man would square off again and again, for as long as the war lasted.

CHAPTER THREE

"I've never been happier to leave a place," Gallo said from his seat aboard the airplane. "Those were some hairy moments. And the Wi-Fi sucked."

"At least we got a deal framework in place," Lewin said from beside him.

"I'll give you that, but I missed a trade opportunity that would have given me a kick-ass slugger. I'll never get out of seventh place."

"There's got to be more to your life than fantasy baseball," she complained.

"And what're your hobbies again? Paperwork, alumni recruiting, and your cat."

"At least when I recruit someone, they actually accomplish something real, not fantasy stats."

The bickering assistants' voices carried through the cabin of the quiet plane. A part of Cap agreed that leaving the battle-stricken Slorenia was for the best. Every time he stepped foot onto their soil, there was bloodshed. Never his intention, it had sadly became his legacy, and one he'd happily put behind him.

While news of the UAV deal was welcomed back home, the press corps traveling with the delegation remained critical of each country's inability to protect American representatives. One even went so far as to suggest that had Captain America not been there, there would have been a loss of life. Also, Scattershot and Psi-Wolf were now more well known than ever before, not something the stealth operatives sought. It did, though, mean, there was increased demand they pay for their attacks, and representatives from each country were meeting with S.H.I.E.L.D.'s Captain Phillips to determine what their options were.

When Cap talked to Sharon Carter that morning, she reported that neither captive had said anything, but both were safely incapacitated and could easily be delivered for a trial should it come to that. She also told him agents were tracking the whereabouts of the other members of the Peristrike group, although their movements implied they were at liberty. It did portend they might be off the board and not a threat. Pessimistically, Rogers worried that they were headed for the Americans' next stop.

Everything suggested Transia was going to feature another attack, but when, by whom, and why remained sheer speculation, only adding to Captain America's tension headache.

He tried to drain his mind of such thoughts and focused instead on the cloudless sky. Losing track of time allowed his mind to settle down and relax for a change, although that ended far too quickly when the unmistakable shape of an imposing mountain could be seen from above.

"Is that it?" Jackson inquired from beside the Avenger.

"Yes, that's Wundagore Mountain."

"Amazing history, that place. I used to read it about during the off-season. Few lands have legends to match that."

While Cap knew of Wundagore's current status, its history was less known to him, so he asked about it.

"You've fought Morgan le Fay, right?"

"Yes, she even managed to shoot me in the shoulder," the hero replied.

"I didn't realize—sorry I brought her up."

Rogers shook his head. "No, go ahead, Senator."

"Al, please. So, Morgan didn't limit herself to England and King Arthur. She was associated with followers of the *Darkhold* and tried to contain a demon they stupidly summoned. When they couldn't do that, they instead trapped it within the mountain. From what I read, and maybe you know better, the demon somehow tainted the soil, and that's where the Puppet Master gathered his clay." The clay from the mountain was imbued with magical energy, allowing Phillip Masters, dubbed the Puppet Master, to form replicas of people and force them to do his bidding.

Cap nodded, thankful he didn't have to contend with that level of threat. "I didn't know that."

"You can't know everything, son. Hell, I can't keep up with half the stuff we're supposed to be 'experts' on in Congress. But this stuff fascinated me so I've kept up with it. Of course, not only does it have magic clay, but that mountain is protected by modern knights, creatures created by the High Evolutionary."

"Okay," Cap said with a chuckle, "that I do know." After all, it was here in the Republic of Transia that Wanda and Pietro Maximoff were born and raised in the shadow of the mountain, not venturing beyond its borders until they were teens. By then, their mutant powers had manifested themselves and they fell under the thrall of Magneto, joining his Brotherhood of Evil Mutants before seeking redemption as the first Avengers Cap was given charge over. Since then, Wundagore's inhabitants had prompted several visits from the Avengers, so he knew the terrain well.

"What about the Russoff curse?" Jackson inquired.

"The werewolf thing? Jack Russell, a descendant of that line, explained it to me once."

"Apparently the male line was cursed centuries ago, and one of the Russoffs even tried to access the *Darkhold* scrolls to lift it," Jackson added.

"I gather that didn't go well."

"Nope."

What Captain America couldn't tell the congressman was that this particular Russoff needed funds and sold a portion of his estate to Jonathan and Meriem Drew, parents to his fellow Avenger Jessica, who fought beside him as Spider-Woman. There was most certainly something about this country that was magical and special and dangerous.

The tiny republic was in the southern Balkans, and shared borders with Macedonia, Latveria, and Transylvania, located almost exactly opposite Symkaria. Recognizing Wundagore's importance, the country's flag featured it as the first in a series of mountain silhouettes under a bright sun.

"What do you hope to accomplish here?" Cap asked. "They have no trade or technology we want."

"No, we're here to extend a hand of friendship. Wundagore has scared off a lot of people, as has Transia's proximity to Latveria. While they have a UN embassy in New York, we don't have much in the way of a relationship. Since we were already in the vicinity, the Foreign Relations Committee simply thought a goodwill visit was in order."

"And I'm the goodwill?"

Jackson smiled at that. "We all are, son."

Later, the delegation was given a huge welcome complete with a band, children holding signs, and an effusive welcome from President Gregor Petrov, a young, vibrant man attired in military uniform. The contingent he led included his attractive wife, Ola, and tween son, Pavel, along with several cabinet ministers. Petrov knew the Americans had high-tech translators at their disposal, but he preferred the human touch. His office assigned them a Romanian translator, someone who had won a contest for the honor, so the delegates welcomed Andreea, a beautiful college student, to the already crowded delegation.

Small villages, frozen in the nineteenth century, wound themselves around Mount Wundagore, but some 90 percent of the population lived in East Transia, the country's capital and sole major city. Cap chuckled to himself as Gallo took one look and complained, again, about the weak Wi-Fi. The country, maybe because of contained mystic energies, or just plain luck, had somehow missed being devastated during the Second World War. He'd never been to the country prior to this first visit as an Avenger.

A fleet of open-air cars were filled with a mix of Americans and Transians. Cap was given a prime spot in the lead car with the president and his family. Gregor Petrov was proud of his English, learned at Oxford, and he showed off by translating for Ola and Pavel, who was already learning English, proudly speaking in both languages. Behind them, Andreea gave a running commentary about the sights to Seaver and Martinez. The distance between the airport and East Transia was short, but they crawled along to allow the people, some who had traveled since dawn, to wave and cheer the Americans. Rarely had the people seen such distinguished visitors, so it was certainly a cause for celebration.

For his part, Cap smiled and waved, trying not to convey that he was tense and expecting an attack at any minute. He couldn't see the Helicarrier, but knew S.H.I.E.L.D. was comfortably nearby.

"We'll be eating *cârnaţi afumaţi* tonight . . . sausage . . ." Pavel said in a rush.

"If this part of the world knows anything, it's how to make a good sausage," Cap said, ruffling the boy's hair.

His eyes rarely left the crowds, searching for anything out of the ordinary. By the time the line of gleaming cars stopped before the presidential palace, he had seen nothing. Not that it meant he would let down his guard.

There was a villa nearby where the Americans were to be housed. The delegates would meet with cabinet ministers over cocktails before the state dinner, followed in the morning by a tour of the country. For a change, the Avenger was free for the afternoon, so he decided to walk around the grounds and look for vulnerabilities. Thankfully, most of the press went in to cover the casual meeting. Harper Simmons, though, hung outside, ostensibly talking to the citizens but clearly keeping an eye on Rogers.

Finally, Cap waited in the courtyard between buildings and confronted the *Guardian* reporter.

"Something on your mind?"

The man was in a bulky jacket with lots of pockets, most of which bulged with one thing or another. He was in a dark

T-shirt, pants, and hiking boots. His eyes had seen plenty through his career, and his reputation was a fairly positive one.

"It doesn't take a genius to know something's up," Simmons said.

"On or off the record?"

"Right now, it's just us. I want to know if I have something to worry about. Ojeda's all about putting on a brave face and Seaver's thinking about a trade deal for his re-election campaign. From what I can tell, Jackson doesn't let much ruffle him, and Martinez sees Russian collusion in everything."

"You think the congressman is being paranoid?"

"Russia is such an easy target considering we're Americans, and the Eastern European section has occasionally been occupied by the Soviets."

"Well, no one has attacked us here . . ."

". . . yet."

"Right. Maybe there won't be one and whatever happened before were isolated incidents."

"You don't really believe that, do you?"

Captain America remained silent.

"Didn't think so. Any idea what's going on?"

"I don't mind saying no, because that's the truth. But if I had a theory, I would keep it to myself for now."

"Think you got lucky with those two?"

They walked around the villa's gardens, which were coming to life in the spring air—a riot of color in a green frame.

"No, they're inexperienced. Lots of power, clearly no real training. One on one was fine."

"But together?"

"It would have been challenging, but they didn't show any real idea of how to fight," Cap said. "Scattershot was all energy for maximum destruction. Psi-Wolf may have the armor, but no feel for using it as a weapon."

"Interesting. So what now?"

"We follow the itinerary and hope for the best."

"Hope is what you do. Me, I look for the reality."

The men completed their circuit of the attractive villa and retired to their separate rooms to get ready for dinner. For Steve Rogers, it was repetitious, something statesmen were accustomed to but that were done with a sense of obligation. He took little pleasure in these affairs, preferring to train, read, or sit with some music from the Great American Songbook. He'd already inquired and was directed to a local gym that would be opened early for him the next day, so he could work out and test his ribs. In the meantime, he took his cleaning kit and did the best he could to repair the damage to his uniform, since he'd only brought the one. Using a special solution T'Challa, the brilliant Wakandan king who battled alongside him as Black Panther, invented for him, he cleaned the shield and added a polymer sealant to help keep it a shining icon.

At dinner, the Sentinel of Liberty was seated next to the Transian minister of defense, a dour, balding, older man who could stand to lose fifty pounds. Between bites of bread and sips of red wine, he engaged Captain America in a discussion of world affairs, displaying a keen understanding of the geopolitical forces at work well beyond his own region.

"What do you think? Can a little spec of country like ours hope to compete against economic behemoths like America and China?"

"Not at all," Cap said sympathetically. "But you don't need to compete against them."

"What do we have to offer? Craftsmanship? *Plăcinte cu brânză dulce*? It is, how you say it, global trade, a unifying economy. We are being left out and left behind."

"You do have tourism going for you."

"Oh sure, come see the birthplace of the High Evolutionary's New Men. The best thing to happen to us was his relocating to the Moon." It was actually Counter-Earth, an identical planet to Earth, but in exact opposite orbit so the two worlds never saw one another except from space, but Cap didn't bother correcting the minister.

"The mountains—yes, including Wundagore—are beautiful," Cap suggested. "You could consider hiking tours? Maybe coupled with food tours? Those are very popular in America."

The minister swallowed the last of his wine, gesturing for more. "What do I know of food tours? Your people have the luxury. Me, I have to keep an eye on Latveria, since who knows when Herr Doom will want to expand his grasp. Or Macedonia, which occasionally eyes us."

"How big is your army?" Cap asked, little caring about the answer but intent on keep the man talking, not drinking.

"State secret," he bellowed with a barking laugh. "Big enough, sure. But the president is cutting my budget, reallocating monies to the police. We've had some recent incidents with terrorist activity."

"Can you work with the police? Is there something we can offer you?" Cap wasn't a diplomat, but if the goal was to offer a hand of friendship, he was determined to do his best.

"You? You carry a nice, shiny target, but just seeing you will make them scurry into the shadows until you leave. They will strike another day."

"The congressmen can discuss what you need back home, and maybe we can send some counter-terrorism advisors to help."

"Like you sent 'advisors' to Iraq or Vietnam?"

"Not like that at all," Cap said, stiffening. While he wasn't thawed during the Vietnam conflict, he had returned to active duty after American forces were sent to Iraq. He had, though, read the military histories as part of his reintroduction to the modern world, with a keen eye toward America's armed forces. Once a solider, always a soldier he had concluded long ago.

The remainder of the evening was similar until the minister began slurring his comments and several of the waitstaff helped him out of the chamber. Rogers received sympathetic looks from Ojeda and Jackson, and a shrug from Seaver. Such was diplomacy.

The following morning, a clear-headed Steve Rogers was in a tank top and sweatpants lifting the maximum weight the gym offered, a mere 450 pounds. It would have to do, and actually meant he wouldn't overdo it, since his ribs protested with every jerk. They were healing, but would be sore for several more days. The other bruises were now merely discolored marks on his arms, neck, and back. None would hinder him whenever the next attack occurred.

Martinez, Jackson, and Ojeda ran on treadmills nearby, admiring how smoothly Rogers worked the equipment. Cap's disciplined routine was a combination of repetitions on the equipment and isometric exercises. At one point, he stretched flat on the floor and raised himself so that the entire weight of his body rested on his fingertips and toes. From there, he swung his body slowly to one side so that his entire weight rested on his left hand and foot with his right hand and leg extended high in the air. After a moment, he lowered his body to the ground and up again, then repeated this on the opposite side. Once he finished five reps on each side, he lowered himself flat on his stomach and relaxed for five counts. Sweating profusely, he sat down to control his breathing. A grayish towel landed on his right shoulder as the others applauded. Ojeda tossed him a water bottle, and he drank in long, steady gulps.

"Bet you can't do that," Ojeda teased Jackson.

"Not even on my best day as a rookie," he admitted.

Martinez, face red from exertion, tried to say something that came out as a gasp as he slowed down and reached for his water bottle.

"That was pretty, uh, impressive," Ojeda admitted.

Steve nodded and toweled himself dry, ready to jump in the shower and then get dressed. There would be the usual tours and meetings, plus the team would enjoy a presentation from a local grammar school.

"What time does the tour start?" Jackson asked Ojeda.

"Martinez's our clock watcher, but he seems a little winded. I believe the president is hosting a light breakfast before—"

Ojeda's words were cut off by a loud crashing sound, like buildings crumbling during an earthquake. To Cap's ears, the noise was more akin to missiles pounding into concrete, steel, and glass. The city, or more likely, the presidential palace, was under attack, earlier than he expected. Grabbing his shield, which he never let out of his sight, he dashed out of the building without taking time to change into his uniform, leaving the others behind. As he hit the street, he heard sirens, screams, and debris crashing to the streets. Cars were demolished, their alarms cut off midblare as their batteries were crushed. He ran toward the devastation as people raced in the opposite direction, none paying any attention to the red, white, and, blue shield he carried.

Rounding one corner, he saw a woman in a purple leather bodysuit, black gloves, and boots, with a whip hanging from her right hip—and on her powerful left bicep was a familiar red band and black swastika inside a white circle. It was Warrior Woman, Julia Koenig, who, like him, had been subjected to a serum that transformed her into the powerhouse before him. And like Steve Rogers, she'd slept for decades in suspended animation before being resurrected at the direction of Axl Nacht, a modern-day fascist. They were both people out of their times, and they resumed their enmity in a new era. The two had clashed repeatedly in the past, although she normally did not operate on her own. In fact, she had been partnered and married to her male counterpart, Master Man, who had stopped cheating death not long before.

Warrior Woman stood at one corner of the palace, literally punching it apart, creating as much chaos as was possible. Her intentions were fairly clear, but why she wasn't going after the president was the immediate question.

This was answered fairly quickly when a gray armored figure emerged from the dust and shadows. The form had a long, gray coat over lightweight armor, along with arm-length gloves and a red cloak. Under one arm was the unconscious president, carried easily. He hadn't yet noticed the shielded warrior, but Cap recognized him as Master Man's successor, Gotteskrieger.

Taking aim, the Star-Spangled Avenger unleashed his shield at Gotteskrieger's legs, hoping to trip him, but while the German stumbled, he didn't fall. Instead, he placed the limp figure of the president on his shoulder and hurled his collapsible battle staff at the unarmed hero. Timing it precisely, Cap reached out and swung his arm, diverting the staff. Now both men were weaponless, but Gotteskrieger had the advantage of the armor, and was more powerful.

"Stop, America! He will die otherwise," Gotteskrieger yelled, his hoarse voice amplified by an internal speaker.

They'd repeatedly exchanged blows in two different eras, perhaps none as damaging as the battle in Italy in 1943, and Steve knew he was in trouble without his chain mail to protect him.

"What do you want, Gotteskrieger?"

"His death," the German said, letting the president's body drop to the ground. For a moment, Captain America thought the Transian dead, but Petrov reacted to the fall. Cap took a brief moment to wonder about the whereabouts of the man's wife and son, but had no time to focus on either. Instead, he surveyed the scene. There was evidence of destruction everywhere, so much so emergency responders couldn't get near the palace. The police were on hand but were aiding in the evacuation, wisely not trying to fire on the attackers. Out of uniform, he might easily be mistaken for a civilian or an enemy combatant, so he hoped the police remained out of the fray.

Warrior Woman's whip coiled around his legs and they flew out from under him as she jerked her weapon backward. He landed on his muscular chest, cutting his chin, his teeth snapping shut. Rolling onto his back, he saw her hefting a large piece of the palace's façade, taking aim at him.

"You will die, too, Captain America!" she shouted in heavily accented English.

As the piece of sandstone hurtled his way, Rogers rolled to his side, grabbed Gotteskrieger's staff, and used it to help himself rise and dodge out of the way. She yanked again, but with his feet planted, he was not giving ground.

"Catch!" a voice yelled and as Cap turned toward it, he saw Jackson, who must have followed him, take aim and hurl the shield toward him as if they were playing Frisbee in the park.

The shield sailed through the air and he effortlessly caught it with his right hand, then jammed it down, pinning the thick whip. The thickly braided rawhide didn't snap in two as he had expected, but she wasn't getting it back without a fight, either.

Warrior Woman dropped her end of the whip in disgust

and stalked toward him, hands forming fists. He estimated he could take several strikes, but without any real protection, it would hurt—a lot.

Gotteskrieger also hunted him, leaving the president on the ground, dust settling on his still form.

The shield on his arm, Rogers stood still, assessing his options. None of them were particularly good ones. In fact all, even trying to run away, were pretty bad ones. There was debris, gushing water, and small fires everywhere he looked, and the terrain would be difficult in his running shoes. Groaning steel indicated the palace's structural integrity was compromised, and he hoped the entire structure didn't come crashing down. The army was rumbling into sight, tank shapes rounding two corners, but they dared not fire with the president present.

The two villains drew closer, she with a malevolent sneer. His armored helmet hid every inch of his face, making him look even less human, but no less menacing.

Cap had one advantage over them both: years of strategic training and hard-won experience. She was a brawler, like her former mate, and he was overly reliant on his armor and brute strength. Neither were particularly gifted tacticians, although he dared not underestimate her. Whatever difference there was in the German version of Professor Erskine's formula, it most certainly enhanced her cognitive skills. In a moment, she might figure out that advantage.

Using peripheral vision, he quickly scanned the surroundings, then ever so slightly bent his knees.

Powerful muscles propelled Rogers up at an angle, and he was suddenly clinging to a second-floor balcony across the street. Once he gained better footing, he leapt up another story. Behind him, the hero heard a grumble of disgust from the woman; he also heard the unmistakable sound of concrete being snapped apart. Something was coming his way, so he did a perfectly executed flip and was now on the roof, looking down at his opponents.

A hunk of palace sailed toward him and he braced himself, then swatted it away with the shield. The impact rattled his arms but it didn't hurt.

Warrior Woman raced across the street, jumping atop a car to gain momentum to give chase. Gotteskrieger was right behind her.

Most of the buildings in the old city were low ones, so he could easily run and leap, putting distance between them. It also gave him a better view of the city and he could lead them away from the government building and toward a less-populated section. He'd given the city map a good look the night before, anticipating such an attack without beginning to guess who might try next.

He had ruled out most European criminals from the S.H.I.E.L.D. databases, and since the files indicated there had been no recent activity on his current foes' part, he had dismissed them without hesitation. Lesson learned for next time.

He just had to ensure there would be a next time.

As Cap ran and jumped to the next rooftop, he heard Warrior Woman make impact and scramble up the building he just vacated. Somewhere behind her, the armored Gotteskrieger was scaling the building, metal hands digging divots in the brick and stone.

He was lighter than they were and, he hoped, faster. Sprinting, his breathing even, Cap leapt from rooftop to rooftop, never breaking stride. He was putting distance between them but could still hear their heavy footfalls and growls of pure rage.

As he leapt from one rooftop, a heavy flower pot sailed into his back, changing his trajectory. He missed his target and started to fall between buildings, realizing he could break a limb if he hit the street. Desperately, he reached out, grabbed a railing, and arced around and through a plate-glass window. His arms and legs were sliced, and his sweatpants torn in spots, but he kept moving. Dashing past a startled woman and her teenaged daughter, he apologized in English, pausing long enough to open a bedroom window before leaping through it and scrambling up to the roof.

Just as he grasped the lip of the roof, a heavy, armored boot crashed down on his left hand. Had he not anticipated such a move, he might have let go. Instead, he heard bones break as the boot ground his fingers into the brickwork.

Warrior Woman reached down and hauled him up with one clean move, dangling him between buildings. Gotteskrieger reared back to deliver a fatal blow, but his steel hand met indestructible shield. The loud clang could be heard for blocks.

While the Teutonic behemoth held him, Gotteskrieger reached to rip the shield from Captain America's grasp, inciting a vicious tug of war.

She swung Cap back and forth, driving his body into the side of the building. He let out a gasp of air and felt his ribs ache, if not crack afresh. If he did not change tactics soon, they would wear him down and possibly kill him, which certainly seemed to be their goal. Whatever their original mission, killing him was likely personal.

Once again, his body was forcefully slammed into the building, and for a moment his vision blacked out.

Another slam and he felt the shield loosen in his grip as consciousness threatened to leave him. Black spots clouded his vision. He needed to make his move quickly.

The next time she swung him back and forth, he took advantage of the momentum and surprised her by swinging his feet higher and into Gotteskrieger, catching him off guard. The armored titan moved backward just enough to allow Cap to hook a leg around the building. He swung his right arm upward, smashing the shield into Warrior Woman's head. While super strong, she was not particularly super dense and the blow staggered her.

This gave him the impetus to continue moving until he was once more on the roof and could face the two from a better position. Not that he had a clue how to take them down.

With a mechanical yell, Gotteskrieger charged him and rather than swerve, duck, or back away, Captain America charged him, and the two wrapped their arms around one another like wrestlers. While Gotteskrieger might have a strength and weight advantage, Cap had flexibility and agility. He had spent years battling the likes of Batroc the Leaper and had learned a few tricks along the way. While they struggled to gain the advantage, Cap surprised his enemies by tugging backward. The two fell to the rooftop but Cap kept the momentum going by flipping the man over him and then over the roof. Gotteskrieger fell three stories to the ground. Cobblestones cracked as the metallic form crashed into the sidewalk and he let out a groan. It would stagger him and maybe chip the finish on the armor, but Cap knew he'd be back. In the meantime, he had to finish Warrior Woman, and fast.

Once more she had the whip in hand, cracking it overhead, sending one end speeding toward Cap. It sliced along his right arm but despite the pain, he did not relinquish the shield. As she pulled the whip back, he charged forward again, headbutting her in the midsection, sending them back several feet. He followed with a vicious right uppercut that connected with her chin and sent her reeling.

He was tired, bleeding, hurt, and running out of ideas.

Warrior Woman looked at the blood from her split lip, licked it, and eyed him. "I will end you," she cried and charged him.

He held the shield before him, prepared to take the impact. At the last moment, he pulled it aside and moved to the left. She rushed past him like a bull and tried to skid to a halt just before she, too, went over the side. The brick crunched as Gotteskrieger clambered up the side of the building.

Warrior Woman bellowed and leapt up at the Avenger, tackling him to the rooftop. The grit and gravel dug into his flesh as she ground him into the roof. Then, her fists pummeled him for a few seconds before he managed to wriggle the shield between them. She continued to pound away, letting his own weapon injure him, wear him down further.

Gotteskrieger crested the rooftop and stalked their way.

A sizzling sound cut through the air and the next thing Cap saw was Gotteskrieger spasmodically jerking, his armor lightly glowing. His cape caught fire and he had to rip it off.

The distraction allowed Captain America to deliver a right cross that pushed Warrior Woman off of him. Scrambling to his feet, the exhausted hero braced himself for whatever came next.

It turned out to be a second blast that staggered Gotteskrieger.

He recognized the energy signature as it cut through the air. Black Widow flipped over the edge of the roof, gracefully landing on the balls of her feet. The wrist gauntlets containing the Widow's Bite sizzled in the air around her, the high-frequency electrostatic bolts of up to thirty thousand volts sounded sweet to his ears.

She gave him a cold grin and he nodded in return.

The two rushed Warrior Woman from different angles, giving her no way to defend herself. Together they beat at her, wearing the German down until she staggered to her feet, upon which Black Widow opened an ampule pulled from her belt. A purplish gas appeared and within seconds Warrior Woman keeled over, unconscious.

"I've got this," Cap called as he headed for Gotteskrieger, who had regained his own footing.

Holding the shield horizontal, he slammed it into the man's neck once, twice. A small fissure opened and Cap seized the opportunity, his cracked fingers tearing the helmet from the rest of the armor, the rent metal screeching in the air. Gotteskrieger stared dazedly at his attacker and Cap reared back and delivered a blow that sent the armored figure to the rooftop. As the body settled, Black Widow walked up and placed a long, cylindrical device at the base of Gotteskrieger's back.

"Localized EMP," she explained. "It will short out whatever tricks are inside the tin can."

"Thanks, Natasha. I had it, though."

"Really?" she cocked an eyebrow at him. "Looked to me like you were running out of gas."

"True, but there's always a way."

"Spoken like a true Boy Scout. Let's get them squared away and go see about the damage."

"Wait, what about the president?"

Black Widow bound Warrior Woman's hands and arms without answering. Captain America strode over and stood above her, looking down, his eyes demanding answers.

"He's fine. His wife and son didn't make it."

"Damn."

The sound of a S.H.I.E.L.D. transport arriving interrupted their conversation. Without waiting for the agents to disembark, Rogers and Black Widow entered the building they had been standing atop and trudged down the stairs, walking slowly and in silence, back to the villa. He ached with every step, and looked forward to getting his wounds dressed and taking a long, hot shower. There might be a gallon of coffee involved, too.

Rogers realized just how far he had led the enemy combatants from the seat of government, but the damage had already been done. Fire trucks, ambulances, police, and the army created a cacophony of sound and clogged most streets. Thankfully, his stature, shield, and black-suited, red-haired companion made him recognizable even out of uniform, and people parted to let them through. Some cheered at the sight of him, and a few paused to shake his hand for stopping the threat. He was thankful he shook with his right hand as his left fingers throbbed in agony, even if he had been trained to ignore the pain. To the Avenger, the entire event was a major failure. Lives had been lost, property damaged, and he had zero clue what was happening and more importantly, why.

No doubt the secretaries of state and defense would want to recall the delegation, which he took to be a personal failing on his part, being unable to properly ensure their safety.

The American media present would also be all over this—a third attack in three cities raised the same questions he had been asking himself. They'd want statements, exclusive interviews, and lots of photos. Worse, the arrival of a fellow Avenger and S.H.I.E.L.D. operative would make it appear that things were escalating or that he could not handle matters on his own and needed help. Considering the adversaries, he was confident enough in his skills to know he could have somehow stopped the German duo, but this way was faster and more efficient. Right now, there were four in custody and it was time to start seeking answers.

The two Avengers were cleared to access the villa where the four delegates and their two aides were clustered in conversation. Police had set up a barrier that the press strained against, shouting questions that they didn't really expect answers to, although, at least for them, hope sprang eternal.

"My god, are you all right?" Ojeda asked as she rushed over.

"I'll live," Rogers told her. "Do you know Agent Romanova?"

"We haven't had the pleasure," the congresswoman said, extending a hand. "Roberta Ojeda, senator from New Mexico."

They shook hands, an entirely normal action amid all the unreal activity.

Briefly, Rogers outlined what had happened, and that S.H.E.I.L.D. now had the pair in custody. Captain Phillips of the *Crescent* had suggested they assign additional agents on the ground to provide the American delegation with increased security. Cap would have preferred to keep it to just himself and Black Widow, but he was responsible for a considerable number of American lives. His instincts said to tough it out with just themselves, but S.H.I.E.L.D. support also made sense.

He was obligated to mention the suggestion to Ojeda, who had the final authority in the matter. When she cocked an eyebrow at him, he said, "We could benefit from additional eyes in the sky at minimum. More boots on the ground just makes us that much bigger a target." He called Phillips and arranged for the Helicarrier to move closer, with drones monitoring the delegation's path.

In turn, Ojeda filled them in on the amount of devastation and where the various ministers were under armed protection. The president, injured but refusing treatment, was with the bodies of his wife and son at the hospital.

"Now what happens?" Black Widow asked.

"That's up to the local government. They could ask to hold the prisoners for trial. They could kick us out for bringing this upon them," Ojeda explained.

"But you didn't bring this on them at all," Cap protested.

"It appears that way. We're trouble magnets. Maybe, they could ask for our help. Right now, no one is talking or making decisions unrelated to the emergency."

"There's little I can do here," Rogers told Ojeda, who nodded. "I'll go get cleaned up."

"You need a doctor."

"I've got him," Romanova said, taking him by the arm and steering him toward the villa's entrance.

"Put him in uniform if possible. We need to show the colors, as it were."

Romanova grimly nodded and steered her charge inside the building. He guided her to his bedroom and once inside, collapsed on the bed face first, letting out a groan of pain and exhaustion. She went over to his S.H.I.E.L.D.-issued first-aid kit and gathered supplies, then began to tenderly clean the cuts, scrapes, and lacerations. She applied special mesh tape that would hold the broken fingers together and help the healing process. His clothes were a total loss, so she used the surgical scissors to slice them off as he remained still, breathing deeply and evenly. At no point did he stir as he hovered so close to sleep or unconsciousness, even he couldn't be certain which it was. Instead, in his mind, he replayed the fight, assessing how he could have handled the two foes differently, not coming up with any good solutions.

Rogers had lost track of the time it took Black Widow to retape his ribs and address the injuries on his chest and shoulders. Clearly, he had passed out, although he still felt exhausted.

"Time?" he murmured.

"Time for some food then a shower," Romanova said. She gestured to a rolling table that was piled with covered plates of local delicacies and a pot of steaming coffee. Slowly, wincing along the way, he sat up and then stood. Once he knew he wouldn't keel over, he hobbled over to the table and sat. She nursed a mug of coffee as he poured his own.

"Thanks," he said as he added some milk. "You know those bruisers?"

"Just from the files, which is enough. Didn't you used to date Warrior Woman in 1942?"

He barked a laugh at that. "Julia and I may have danced, but we never dated. Besides, Hitler had her married to Master Man, and I am too much the gentleman to date a married woman."

"But Master Man died. She's available," Natasha Romanova teased.

Rogers uncovered a plate, recognized eggs and some of the vegetables, and heaped most of it onto his plate. "Yeah, Nacht's father was a part of their super-solider program and turned Wilhelm Lohmer into Master Man. Strucker had them both suspended until Nacht brought them back to life. Did you know Nacht fell in love with Julia's picture and had himself subjected to the treatment to be worthy of her?"

"What men won't do for sex," Romanova said.

"Lohmer surprised them both. After losing his super strength, he was a frail old man and sacrificed himself to stop Nacht and Julia."

"You were there, right?"

"Yes," he said between mouthfuls. He ate mechanically and steadily, not really tasting the food but refueling and brooding. "I was with Namor and the original Torch, the Invaders reunited."

It never ceased to amaze him how so many of his former comrades in arms had survived the war and were still active today. Battling Warrior Woman on those rooftops, with their antiquated architecture, made it feel like they could have been fighting back in 1943.

"Is S.H.I.EL.D. able to hold all four of them?" he asked, changing the subject and switching from eggs to sausage, recalling what Pavel, now dead, had said about them.

"Farrell's good, don't worry, Steve," she said.

"That's a lot of firepower to contain," he countered.

"True, but as long as no one tries to free them from the Helicarrier, they should be fine. I suspect none of these countries wants them on hand for trial—not without you or someone powerful enough to contain them."

"Could all four go to the ICC?"

"Maybe, but that's above our pay grade. Eat up so you can go clean up."

Rogers nodded, losing himself in thought about what he could have done differently, and failing to take satisfaction in knowing he did his best.

CHAPTER FOUR

An hour later, a uniformed Steve Rogers and Black Widow were walking the countryside, away from East Transia and toward the small villages ringing Wundagore Mountain, which ominously overshadowed the region. Stretching his muscles felt good, but Cap knew he was far from combat ready. He continued to fret over the last several days and the illogic of the attacks.

"I never did ask you, what brought you to Transia?"

"Sharon."

"She's worried about me?"

"Steve, she's always worried about you. The frequency of attacks made it sound like something bigger was brewing and she asked me to look into it."

Gesturing beyond the mountains, Rogers said, "Every time I come here, I fight. I did it during the Second World War, and I've done it ever since. I've spilled blood here and haven't thought twice about it until now."

"The boy? The mother?"

"He didn't ask for his father to be president or to live in some small country that someone wants. Their ancestors fought for Russia, which means they were against us, then with us, then the Iron Curtain fell and they were our enemy again. The borders in Eastern Europe are drawn with cotton candy, easily dissolved and remade."

"I'm aware of that, you know," she reminded him. "We were drilled on geography as part of our training, unlike most of the world, which continues to confuse Transia with Transylvania and worry Dracula still lives here."

He chuckled and said, "We know better."

"That we do. But Steve, these people are not out to spread ideology. They want to live, raise their families, and be left alone."

"So do the people of Symkaria and Slorenia. They're all tiny, struggling economies in a world that swings from globalization to protectionism and isolation. Sooner or later, they're going to get swallowed up or crumble."

"You're worried they're going to be annexed?"

"Well, your home country seizes opportunities . . ." he began but stopped himself. He was many things but a global strategist was not one of them. Geopolitics was intel he needed for mission specifics and, given their ever-shifting natures, were abstractions that hurt his head. Shifting topics slightly, he added, "Then you add in the heightened ethnic or religious strife and these people don't stand a chance.

Slorenia remains ready to crack apart because of those ideological differences."

"You just want to buy everyone a Coke and teach them to live in perfect harmony," she chided.

"I know it's idealistic and even simplistic, but we've been at one another's throats over ideas and concepts rather than just accepting there is more than one way to view the world."

"You'd put yourself out of a job."

"I'd be okay with that."

"And do what? I'm a spy, there's always going to be need for me even when we're living in harmony. I'd help ensure it."

"I'm an artist, I could go sit behind an easel or drawing board," he reminded her.

"How come you never sketch me?"

"I could when this is over, if you'd like. I hope to have some leave when we get home."

Cap walked farther, reaching a crest in the path that overlooked a small valley that made Wundagore and its sister mountains look even larger.

"The Balkans have been fought over for millennia," Black Widow said, her tone more serious. "It's funny considering how mineral poor the land is, how bad for agriculture it can be. Instead, the mountains formed defenses and the wood was good for building. We had access to the Black Sea and people could sail and trade. It's one reason they're seen as backward or antiquated. The frequent wars, changing of governments, and lack of resources meant the people were always struggling. So many dialects to learn, so many leaders to revere one day and hate another.

"It's one reason why there's so little trust here. That extends all the way north and across Russia. It's a hard land, a hard life, so you fight to keep what's yours and presume the worst in others."

Cap remained silent, taking in the landscape, the sun just beginning to dip behind the most distant portion of the range.

"Distrust is ingrained in us. We were never to question our teachers or think about ideology, just our missions." And few would know that better than Romanova. She'd grown up in the Red Room, a Cold War–era program where twenty-eight orphaned girls were turned into biochemically enhanced, deadly weapons, complete with false memories implanted in their minds. Natasha Romanova was the best of the bunch, earning the title of Black Widow, and was sent to America to begin her career, first as an assassin, then a spy.

"How did you learn to trust anyone, then?"

"Being in America was unlike anything I had experienced before, so I immersed myself in your media with all its freedoms. And of course, there was Clint."

Clint Barton, former circus performer, one-time criminal,

and adventurer who fought with Captain America as Hawkeye. Like the Maximoffs, he sought redemption by joining the Avengers and proved to be among their bravest members. Early on, Black Widow convinced Barton to join her on a mission that put them in conflict with Iron Man, her first major defeat. Their partnership evolved into a brief romance before settling into a deep and abiding friendship.

"I saw things to fight for, not to be scared of," she continued. "The people here, they fight out of fear of being overrun. Their families have handed down countless horror stories stretching back beyond the Ottoman Empire. Add the monstrous activity in Wundagore, and you have plenty to be frightened of and little to take pride in."

"So why try and assassinate the president?"

"I don't know. It might not have been an assassination attempt, since the other attacks were on buildings. He may have been collateral damage or a miscalculation. But I'd like to stay and help you figure this out."

Rogers clapped a hand on her shoulder without looking away from the landscape. "I appreciate it, Natasha."

"Sharon thinks there's a pattern," she said as she got them walking again, this time back toward the capital.

"What sort of pattern?"

"None of the attacks were directed at you or the congressmen, but were timed for your presence in each country. In every case, it was to cause mayhem and destruction but not

ROBERT GREENBERGER

outright assassination or even a coup. The very randomness suggests a pattern."

"Two Russian agents, two German, is that part of the pattern, too?"

"Maybe. Think about this: all four are what you and I would consider low-level operatives. Seldom seen. Each were without their allies. The rest of Peristrike Force has not been seen, nor has the Axis Mundi that Gotteskrieger and Warrior Woman belong to."

"Meaning what?"

"I'm not sure, which is why I'm sticking around."

Each were left to their own thoughts as they worked their way back to the remains of the palace. For Rogers, it was a chance to filter Romanova's ideas with his own experiences and try to find more to the situation. He trusted Sharon Carter, his lover, ally, and current director of this mission. If she saw a pattern, then there had to be one, but the hidden hand and the rationale remained elusive, gnawing away at him. Between that and the aches, he suspected sleep would be challenging later.

Eventually, they returned to the capital, people giving the uniformed foreigners a wide berth. Most had donned black armbands or clothing out of respect for the president's double loss. Flags were already flying at half mast and the streets were eerily quiet, with little noise beyond a few motor vehicles and yapping dogs. The worst was over and it was time, once more, to pick up from a battle. While the majority of Transia's people had not been to war, they knew their country's history all too well.

Police tape surrounded the streets, and armed patrolmen framed the capital and villa at every corner. Vehicular traffic had been rerouted but construction crews had yet to come and begin clearing the debris. Voices were hushed as they passed and few met their eyes as the attack's consequences settled over the populace.

Entering the villa, the pair headed for the vast lobby where Jackson and Seaver huddled over a laptop looking over research in preparation for a meeting, adhering to an agenda in danger of disintegrating.

Gallo and Lewin were on their phones while Martinez spoke with a local reporter. Only Ojeda, their leader, was absent. Empty paper cups and plates of half-eaten food littered several tables and there was a general malaise over the room.

Once Seaver spotted Captain America and Black Widow, he rose, catching everyone else's attention. One by one, they drifted toward the pair, none looking thrilled.

"What's the situation?" Cap asked.

"Roberta is on the phone with the White House and we've been asked to remain indoors for now," Seaver said, his drawl more pronounced. "Me, I'm hoping we stay the course. Show strength."

"The president?"

"Home, being watched over. The country has announced a three-day period of mourning so things are grinding to a halt."

"But no martial law?" Black Widow asked.

"No, they all seem to realize the threat came and went."

"That's something," Cap said.

"Captain, do you have any answers?" Jackson said.

"Not yet. Probably have the same number of questions you do," he answered.

"The press spoke to all of us, now they want you," Martinez said. "The government is keeping their own media at bay, so everyone is going to get the story from our press."

"Should I do it?" he asked, clearly not looking forward to the questions, especially the ones he couldn't answer.

"If you don't, it looks like we have something to hide," Jackson said.

"We don't, right?" Seaver asked, eyeing Black Widow.

"Congressman, Black Widow is here as a fellow Avenger, supporting me. If anything, a Russian hero might go some way toward calming suspicions."

"She here as an Avenger or a S.H.I.E.L.D. agent?" Seaver asked.

"I'm here because the situation calls for it," Romanova replied. "I am not here to talk to the press."

"You've been seen," Jackson said. "They know you're here."

"It doesn't mean I have to talk to them. Cap should handle it."

"Fine. Set it up and I'll do what I can," Cap told them. At those words, Gallo spun on his heel and headed toward the adjacent conference room where the press was holed up. To Cap, it was like keeping specimens in a lab, allowing them to fester and grow into something malignant. They would want answers he didn't possess and then get confrontational, especially Simmons and Singer. Still, this was why he was there and he'd have to do his best.

At Gallo's wave, he knew they were ready for him. Squaring his shoulders, he marched toward the media, feeling not unlike a lion being led into the Coliseum.

The questions began even as Gallo ushered Cap into the smaller space. It smelled of burned coffee with a dose of fear. Cap stood ramrod straight, projecting a confidence he didn't entirely feel and waited for things to settle.

"Yo, guys, lower it," Gallo shouted and the media finally settled.

Captain America took his position on one side of a large, highly polished wooden table. It was massive and weighty with ornate carvings at each corner, speaking of an earlier age. Atop it were cell phones, digital recorders, and one device on a small tripod. Other reporters held up their gadgets of choice to capture every word, every exchange.

He gestured to Amberson, the friendliest one in the room.

"Who were they? What did they want?"

"Good questions, Mr. Amberson," Cap began and detailed the public information about the two Nazi fascists. Amberson asked a followup about Cap's past dealings with the female foe, confirming this was the same person. Some things Cap held back—information not yet declassified or germane to the moment.

"Following up on that," Singer interrupted, "you didn't say what they wanted." Rogers noted the other reporters had yet to warm to her abrasive nature and gave her dirty looks.

"Because, Ms. Singer, we don't know. Like Scattershot and Psi-Wolf, they did not announce their intentions."

"Do you have a guess?"

"I try not to guess," he began, frowning at the question. "We have three attacks by four enemies. They have not been previously linked, nor is there an obvious connection between the three countries beyond geography."

Norah Winters, who had made her name with *Front Line* during the civil war that nearly split the heroic community, gestured and was next.

"Is the American delegation in danger?"

"At no point were they targeted, as I am sure you noticed," Rogers replied. The question was just to get him on the record regarding the obvious, but still, it irked him.

"Following up," Singer interrupted once more. "After these attacks, can you assure their safety?"

"Of course," he said with as much confidence as he could muster.

"Have you been injured in these fights? Your fingers are taped. Are you at your peak?"

He bristled at that and considered ways of obfuscating the issue but had to give her something. "In any battle, there are injuries, but as you can see, I remain ready to serve."

"Then why is Black Widow now here?"

"She has volunteered her time to lend tactical support to the investigation, not the protection of the congressmen."

"How familiar is she with this area? She's Russian, right?" Simmons asked.

"Her activities have had her pretty much around the world. Perhaps she has yet to visit Micronesia, but she'll get there," he said with a smile, hoping to lighten the mood.

"Can you guarantee the safety of the Transians?" Singer asked.

"We believe the threat has been handled," he said. "As in the other countries, once the first attack was stopped, there have been no followups."

"What about Slorenia?" Winters asked. "That's our next stop, right?"

"According to the itinerary, yes. But obviously, we're reviewing everything."

"So, there's a chance we might go home?" Singer said, just ahead of Winters, who shot her a dirty look.

"Congresswoman Ojeda is talking to Washington right now and we should have confirmation about our plans later today."

"Are you worried about a fourth attack?" Amberson asked.

"Given the pattern so far, of course there is an increased chance of an attack," Cap said, starting to feel uncomfortable. At first he ascribed it to the questions, but then he realized whatever painkillers Romanova had given him were wearing off.

"Shouldn't the congressmen want to avoid subjecting the Slorenians to danger?"

"As I said, Ms. Winters, these attacks were not aimed at Americans, so might happen whether we are present or not."

"But the timing . . ." Singer started again.

"Yes, more than coincidental," he told her.

"Wouldn't they be safer then by not going?"

Cap hesitated, biting back a sharp retort. Just then, the door opened and Ojeda walked in. Cap couldn't read her professional, neutral expression but stepped aside to give her the floor.

"Ladies and gentleman, I have just gotten off the phone with the White House. It has been reaffirmed that Americans do not cower. We will maintain our schedule with one adjustment and that is to return here to represent America at the funeral of President Petrov's wife and son."

"What if there's a new attack? Can Transia withstand a second one in so short a time?" Singer jumped in.

"This country has endured much, but there is nothing to suggest a second attack is imminent, so your baseless speculation is inappropriate," Ojeda said.

She gave Cap a minute nod of her head and the two walked out of the conference room, leaving the press corps to figure out what story to spin. Several final questions were uttered without reply.

Wincing as he moved, Captain America wondered if *he'd* be prepared for another attack anywhere.

"We've got to stop meeting like this," Nick Fury told Steve Rogers.

The two soldiers were seated side by side in a bar on the outskirts of Germany. It was not far from the Allied camp where Fury and his men were currently posted. Rogers had arranged the meeting through Allied Command days earlier. Both men looked ragged, dark rings under their eyes, Fury with a two-day old beard. They were battle-tested, hardened men who thought they had seen everything but were regularly proven incorrect.

Rogers nursed his beer while Fury signaled for his second. Around the bar, small groups of weary men on a brief break mixed with the few locals who dared be seen with Americans.

"You know, I thought once Mussolini gave up, we were close to the end," Rogers said.

"Wouldn't that be nice, but Adolf's had other ideas. Some pretty scary ones, too."

"That's what I'm here about," Rogers told Fury, then took a sip.

"Lemme guess, they've gone out and started building their own monsters, like Frankenstein," Fury said with a harsh laugh.

"Thankfully, no."

"Okay, you got me curious, Cap, what's up?"

"Project Lazarus."

Fury didn't surprise easily, less so with every passing day, but his eyes went wide at the name of the German operation. Fury's company had aided Captain America and Bucky in smashing the operation, located at Drache Castle. Dr. Nikolaus Geist had been one of the powers behind Hitler's rise in German politics, and his scientific expertise rivaled that of Professor Erskine or Phineas Horton, but Geist was out for power and influence, not to benefit mankind. With losses mounting, Hitler asked for help and Geist came up with Lazarus, a way to resurrect the honored dead, imbuing them with enhanced strength and durability, their decayed minds easily manipulated. While Captain America and Bucky managed to stop the program before it got out of control, the Howling Commandos provided backup and ultimately mop-up support.

"They resurrect your dancing partner Erklin?"

"Thankfully, no. Instead, it seems a few of those men ran off with Strucker and Geist. We never could find the formula or the records. Now we've learned Strucker has them and is building a new stronghold."

"Where?"

"Alberia."

"They're neutral," Fury objected.

"You think a country's neutrality would stop Strucker? It's a perfect cover if the government doesn't know about it."

"Which they don't."

Rogers finished his beer and nodded once. "Our job, Nick, is to find Strucker and destroy the notes."

Fury eyed him a long time before saying anything. "Did intelligence really want those notes destroyed?"

"It's a sin to raise the dead. It's one thing to build super humans like me and Lohmer, but it's something else entirely when dealing with those who died. What's lost in battle can't be re-created."

"You getting enough sleep?"

"No, and neither are you. I'll get a long nap when the war's over," Rogers assured him. They'd fought numerous times side by side and Rogers had come to trust Fury with his life. It was why he admitted he was tweaking the orders. He knew that if anyone got the notes and re-created the formula, the temptation would be too strong not to use it again. No, in his mind, it had to be ended. Geist was a danger, but his handler, Strucker, was a zealot, a true threat to democracy. Strucker's power in the Nazi Party was second only to the Red Skull's and it was clear he saw the writing on the wall. His estimates were off, but clearly, the Allies were going to win the European war and then go east and deal with Japan. Strucker, like a good squirrel, was storing things away for the coming cold winter.

"Understood, Captain," Fury said, rising from the barstool. "Just say when and where. We'll be ready."

Rogers rose, shook Fury's hand, and assured him the orders were forthcoming.

Two days later, Captain America, Bucky, and Fury's Howling Commandos crossed the border into Alberia, a Central European country set in the Northwestern Tatras and rich in agriculture that survived the war by allowing all sides to cross their borders. They were tiny and not worth conquering. Since everyone needed food, the visitors paid and the soldiers left the fields alone. It was perhaps the country's best economic period after a century of privation.

There was a little-used, mostly dirt road that was largely covered by foliage. It was here that the American men carefully marched into the neutral territory. There were known warrens of caves within the base of the mountains—where better to hide the reanimated dead and their bible than in cool caves, away from prying eyes?

"Strucker's up to something," Fury said.

"He's always up to something," Cap said. "You've exchanged shots with him before, what do you think?"

Captain America had taken point and Fury kept him company while the rest of the commandos walked single file. Bucky was four men back, talking jazz with Gabe Jones.

The war seemed to age Bucky, hardening him in unimagined ways, hence his preference for using guns. He needed an edge, Bucky argued, since he lacked a one-of-a-kind shield and a super-soldier formula, and Cap couldn't counter. He hoped that once the war ended, Bucky could reclaim what was left of his teenage years and enjoy life a little, find a girl, go to college.

"After he lost one fight too many, Hitler effectively demoted him. Word is, he and the Skull have been planning something. I hear tell he was in Japan not too long ago and has been coming and going all around Germany ever since."

"A weapon?"

"Something like that, but it has to be designed for use after Hitler falls. We all see that coming and Strucker's a loser, but he's no fool. He's got some operation being built, something deeper and nastier than the Nazis."

"You think Geist is a part of that? Him and these ghouls?"

"I don't know, but he's hiding all this away, so that says something."

Cap was about to say something when he was shushed by Dum Dum Dugan, the beefy red-haired Irishman who somehow got away with wearing a bowler instead of a GI–issued helmet. Dugan gestured with his fingers and Fury nodded in understanding. Cap figured out that someone or something was up ahead, not far from the first of the Tatras in the area.

Fury motioned for Izzy Cohen and Dino Manelli to fan left, Bucky and Gabe Jones to the right. As they faded from sight, several of the others, including Rebel Ralston, Pinky Pinkerton, and Eric Koenig, filled the gap, backing Cap and Fury.

Jones returned a few moments later, letting the men know that two armed enemy targets were in that direction. With a nod, Fury sent Pinkerton to retrieve Cohen and Manelli, then indicated he'd go forward with Cap behind him.

There was an easy feel among the men, who were always cracking wise and never looking like they took the war too seriously. That was to underestimate how Fury had trained them to become an unstoppable fighting machine. Sure, they'd lost men along the way, but their core was intact and their reputation worked to their advantage. Hitler hated few Americans more than the cluster now walking around Alberia.

As they emerged from the last of the trees that lined the near-forgotten road, they were exposed by a crescent moon–lit sky. It was partly cloudy, dim, but not pitch black. It was cold enough that they could see their breath, but none wore coats for fear of encumbering their movements. Across the stretch of land between the trees and the base of the mountain were half a dozen shambling shapes. Two were in Nazi uniform while the other four were in overalls. It was clear to Cap that Geist had gone back to work on his formula, and was now using Alberian natives as test subjects. All six carried rifles, and one also carried a pitchfork.

Fury raised a fist to halt all movement as he assessed the situation. Captain America knew they'd be smarter than these soldiers—he could match their strength and they had the accuracy of his fellow soldiers' weapons. Their enemies were dead already, so killing them again did not weigh on his conscience. Fury's fingers drove the men quickly into position, but not quietly enough as someone cracked a fallen branch with his boot.

All six reanimated men turned at once, spotted the commandos, and raised their weapons. No one appeared to be in command and yet they all moved with uncanny speed and precision, even the farmer.

"Cut 'em down," Fury cried.

Gunfire from both sides shattered the still night air. Fury's men fired once and fell to the ground, seeking cover where possible. Bucky held the rifle to his shoulder, exposed to the dead, and blasted once, then twice, before crouching. Two of the farmers fell, two more took hits and fell back. One of the Nazi soldiers shot and stepped back, shot then stepped back. Pinky Pinkerton, their sole British member, yelled in pain. Instantly, Danny Visentin was at his side, his medic's kit coming into view. Cap heard the covering fire letting the enemy men fall back, toward the mountain. Still, the commandos easily outnumbered them.

Fury called out, "Reed, Strell, Gentile—covering fire. Jones, Dugan, Manelli, with me!" Instantly, the three men shot at the retreating figures, letting the others duckwalk their way forward. Manelli stepped on an unseen rock, lost his footing and fell over, yelping in pain. The farmer with the pitchfork saw that, and hurled the tool at the fallen man.

Captain America's shield sailed through the air, meeting the tool five feet from the downed solider. Covering fire flanked him as he dashed to collect Manelli, who clearly couldn't get back up.

"Bucky, get him back to the tree line," he ordered.

"It's just a twisted ankle, Cap, I'm good to go," Manelli protested.

"We have enough men, so protect yourself," Cap insisted and turned away, hustling back to Fury. Within seconds, the remainder of the reanimated men were cut down.

Cap and Fury stood over the bodies while the rest of the Howling Commandos spread out, forming a protective curtain.

"They gave us more of a fight at the castle," Fury said.

"Something's wrong with the formula. Maybe he changed it and weakened it in the process. We need those notes, Nick."

"I bet they're in there," Fury said, gesturing at the first cave mouth.

"I'll take that bet. And raise you that they're not unprotected."

"How do you want to play this?"

"You said it the other day, we're tired. Let's do this fast and hard and get out of here. We're not exactly invited guests."

"Jones, round up everyone who can stand and split into two teams. Flank the mountain entrance. You'll be exposed, can't be helped, but you outgun them."

You hope, Cap thought.

"Dugan, Bucky, you're with us," Fury said, slipping the rifle from his shoulder as he made a direct line for the cave entrance.

"Flashlight," Fury said and suddenly one was in his hand. Dugan seemed to have pockets for everything.

As they neared the opening, the four paused. Cap couldn't hear, see, or smell anything, but that did not mean they were safe. He picked up a rock and threw it deep into the cave where it bounced off a rocky wall, making a distant clicking sound. Nothing.

Fury nodded and switched on the light, shining it around the cave. The first thing he saw was a reflection—training the light, he saw it was a thin metal pipe with several tanks at one end and the other trailing out of sight. He flashed the light deeper and spotted twin filing cabinets. Slowly, Fury went deeper inside the cave, Cap right beside him, Dugan and Bucky spread a little to either side.

They saw a makeshift lab, similar to the one they had destroyed at the German castle. A body was on one table, covered by a sheet, with electrodes, wires, and a catheter attached to it. Three blackboards were farther back, covered in Geist's manic scrawl. No one could make out the symbols or formulae that had been written. Fury paused and shone the light past all that, deeper into the cave.

A screaming Nazi soldier with wild eyes hurtled at them as if shot from a cannon. He'd been waiting deep in the cave's recesses, luring the Americans out of sight of the ones guarding the cave entrance. He was large and broad, heavy-set, and Cap instinctively knew he'd be powerful.

Before he could position himself, the reanimated Nazi was upon him, the two falling to the dirt, grappling. While not in Master Man's class, the Nazi was stronger than any opponent Cap had fought before. To confirm that, the creature delivered a punch to Cap's solar plexus that *hurt*. The Nazi followed that up with a quick left-right combination that left Cap staggered. He tried to bring up his left arm to use the shield for protection, but the Nazi punched him hard once more then scrambled over him, pinning the arm against the hard-packed ground.

Rogers wondered why Fury, Dugan, and Bucky weren't helping, but he heard sounds of fists hitting flesh, boots scraping the dirt and knew the three were otherwise occupied. It was up to him to stop this one and then help the others, who might well be overmatched.

By moving up to pin his arm, the Nazi left Cap's legs

free, so he hooked them around his attacker and used those powerful muscles to peel his opponent away from his body. With his right arm out, he rose and delivered a crushing blow to the man's face. With the Nazi now off him, Cap got up, grabbed the man's collar, and rammed his head into the rock wall, then twisted the man's neck until he heard the crack of bone. The body instantly went limp.

Catching his breath, he saw Dugan about to be pummeled so ran over and let the attacker's fist meet his shield. That allowed Dugan a chance to withdraw his pistol and empty it into the man's head.

At much the same time, Fury and Bucky were trading dance partners, a vicious combination of punches and kicks that kept the two reanimated men banging into one another. There was a determined look in Fury's eye and a wicked grin on Bucky's face, not that Cap believed either was enjoying himself. But once the threat was ended, they breathed hard and tense, certain they were not done.

"They were hiding in here to protect the files?" Fury asked.

"Or to protect Geist," Dugan said.

Captain America paused to take it all in, his mind turning over the possibilities. There was no evidence of Strucker nor any sign people lived in this particular cave. In fact, it looked like a lab, and not even the primary one given the rudimentary layout and equipment.

"It's fake," he declared.

Bucky walked over to the filing cabinets and opened them. Pulling out a folder, he saw papers but grimaced in the dim light. "Fuel consumption reports," he said. "These are from some depot."

"What about the blackboards?"

"Were we to haul those back, some scientist will tell us it's the formula for chocolate or penicillin. It's like a movie set," Cap said bitterly.

"Leaked intel to lure us here," Fury said. "All designed to pull us away from Strucker's real trail, delay us, and maybe kill us with these guards."

For a long while, the four men stood in silence, the air hanging heavy with the disappointment each felt.

"Every time we knock down the Skull or Strucker or Master Man they come back," Cap finally said softly, the weariness evident in his voice.

"While those yahoos get away, we're making progress against Hitler's goons," Dugan said, trying to lighten the mood.

"But now there are dead Nazis to fight, too," Bucky said.

"I think that threat's over with Geist in the wind," Cap assured him. "Still, I thought . . . I hoped the war would end last year. And here we are, 1944 almost over and we're still at it. This last act is feeling drawn out and endless."

"We'll get 'em, Cap," Fury said. "Remember, we're the good guys."

CHAPTER FIVE

The mood was somber as Captain America and Black Widow sat alone in the conference room. A pot of coffee, two half-filled cups, and a platter of assorted baked goods sat between them. Cap looked out the window, letting his mind wander, as Black Widow gripped the armrests and knit her brow in concentration. They'd been like that for some time.

"It makes no sense," he finally said, shattering the silence. "The first rule, I thought, was to figure out who benefits, but in this case, it seems no one."

Romanova nodded once then turned to look at him as he turned his gaze toward her.

"Symkaria, Transia, and Slorenia are not contiguous. Neither is the next stop, Carnelia. Other than Russia, they do not appear to have a common enemy. Each is poor and each seems in need of international support in some way. Symkaria is the most technologically advanced while Transia could be if the High Evolutionary was willing to share. None of this adds up to anything obvious."

"Steve, S.H.I.E.L.D. has found nothing to link the attackers, either. They're all threats to one degree or another, but none of us take them all that seriously. Not when we have the shadow of Latveria nearby. But this is not at all how Doom works."

"Are they still digging?"

"Of course. There are forensic accountants trying to find financial links because everyone thinks they were all hired. They have no patriotic links to these countries or an ideology that explains the attacks."

Steve brought his hands heavily down on the tabletop. "This is driving me crazy, Natasha. How can I protect the delegation when I have no idea who's behind it and who may attack next? There has to be a clue here, somewhere."

She took a sip of the now-cold coffee and grimaced.

"What does Ojeda want to do?"

"We're Americans, we don't back away from terrorists," he said.

"Is that you or her?"

"Both, to be honest. We cancel this and it hurts our standing. And, frankly, she thinks we can trade with them and benefit these countries. I admire the goal."

"Peel away the political fallout for a moment, Steve. Let's be practical here. Can you and I properly protect the congressmen and the press from the rest of Peristrike Force or Axis Mundi?"

"We've already fought Warrior Woman and Gotteskrieger, so that just leaves Baroness Blood."

"Is she still active?"

"We can check because, to be honest, I can't keep track of them all."

"Tell me about it. And what about the Force?"

"A few members, but Sharon assured me when Scattershot first attacked, the others were spoken for."

Romanova nodded at that, still frowning. "I still don't like it. Someone is pulling the strings and has resources. We have no real clue who it might be."

"I think we can rule out Paste Pot Pete," Cap said with a smile. Even Black Widow grinned at that.

"Can we linger here, for the funeral, and buy some time to properly scout Carnelia? Delay the trip by a day or two?"

"We can ask Ojeda, but she seems pretty determined to see this through. Seaver is driving the schedule, something about being home on time for committee meetings and votes."

"That's crazy," she said flatly. "We have too many wild cards and we can't be properly prepared. American lives are being put needlessly at risk."

"I have my orders," he said.

She leaned in close, meeting his eyes, now in shadow. "You've defied orders before and with less obvious justification. Do you really think anyone back in Washington would really want the congressmen at risk?"

"The Americans are bystanders," he said quietly. "They are not targets."

"Bystanders get hurt, Steve," she said. "All too often. And you know that. Really, why are you so set on staying here when all logic says bring them home until this blows over."

"I've never backed away from a fight."

"Yes, you're one of the smartest, bravest men I have ever fought alongside. And as the Avengers' most trustworthy leader, you know full well this is a mistake."

"Natasha, if I take them home, and if you're right that they aren't the targets, then the targets remain here, vulnerable."

"So you really want to risk their lives so *you* can be on hand to protect everyone, one country at a time. Do you know how brave—and utterly foolish—that sounds?"

"I can't leave them at risk, Natasha. I just can't."

"Aren't you inserting yourself into sovereign affairs? I know S.H.I.E.L.D. does it with impunity, but seriously, you can't protect seven and a half billion people."

"I can try."

She nodded but he could tell she wasn't sold on the idea. Normally, she was cold and practical, which made her an excellent field operative and team leader. He'd seen her as both through the years, and while they were friends, it was not a close bond, other than their shared affection for Bucky Barnes. Her own Russian training had included impressive drug treatments that severely retarded her aging, meaning she was a young girl in the 1950s when Barnes—saved from the exploding airplane that sent Steve Rogers to his icy sleep, and then brainwashed into being the Winter Soldier—was her instructor and much later, briefly her lover. The Winter Soldier, Cap's old friend, was once more clear headed and fighting the good fight while still dealing with the demons in his mind. Rogers briefly considered calling Barnes in for support but chose not to, considering Black Widow's presence might be more distracting than necessary.

Still, he missed fighting alongside James Buchanan Barnes.

Black Widow herself had her own issues to deal with, he knew. They all did. How they dealt with them was what separated hero from villain. He had watched with justifiable pride how one person after another realized they were on the wrong side of an issue and had worked toward redemption and renewal. Some of his proudest moments were when he helped Hawkeye, the Scarlet Witch, and Quicksilver begin new chapters, enduring public scorn while he led them as the second iteration of the Avengers. Soon after, Hawkeye's romantic partner, Black Widow, saw the Cold War tensions were outdated and shifted her allegiance, first as an Avenger and then as a trusted agent for S.H.I.E.L.D. How many more could be coaxed from the dark into the light?

Rogers rose and opened the door, gesturing to the Slorenian military guard that he'd like to see Congresswoman Ojeda. The man curtly nodded and raised a cell phone to relay the instruction. Within minutes, Ojeda, looking slightly haggard, entered the room and took a chair to Cap's right, close to the window.

"How are you holding up?"

"This has been a nightmare," she said. "We've made some progress on our agenda, of course, but the attacks overshadow everything we've tried to do. We're getting beaten up by the cable news pundits and State is debating summoning us home, overruling the White House chief of staff."

"That's why I asked to see you," Rogers said. "We've been discussing what to do next. Carnelia is in somewhat better shape than here, but the government is still rebuilding. We have concerns over security, so what we'd like to suggest is prolonging our stay here so Black Widow and I can go ahead and make certain things are safe."

Ojeda shook her head slowly. "This country is in mourning. The president is inconsolable, and our presence would only amplify that grief. We can come back for the funeral if we're still welcome, but for now, we need to stick to the itinerary."

"Congresswoman, do you think the State Department may have a point?" Romanova asked. "Three countries, three attacks—it just guarantees there will be a fourth. The loss of life is mounting."

"Ms. Romanova, I have been in contact with the president and for a change we agree. America cannot be seen to be backing down. He's overruled the secretary once and is letting me make the call. And we're going on to Carnelia."

"Do they even still want us there?" Cap asked.

"Prime Minister Nina Krilova called earlier and was most insistent that we consider the invitation still open. She's got her own agenda and needs to show us off to her people."

Cap grunted at that, an involuntary sound, nodding.

"S.H.I.E.L.D. still has a Helicarrier in the region, so they can provide additional support. In fact, I'll ask them to go ahead and begin scouting on your behalf. But I agree with Captain America; this will be seen as provocative. We can do our best to protect you, but as you can see, lives will certainly be lost," Black Widow said, making her point clear.

"We're not the targets are we?"

"No, ma'am, we're not," Rogers said.

"I know the timing makes us look bad, but someone wants something with these countries. We're either here to bear witness or are somehow involved. Have you any further thoughts as to who may be behind it? Doom? The Red Skull? Hydra?"

"All ruled out," he assured her. He was, frankly, just as glad it was not Doctor Doom, ruler of Latveria. His desire for global domination likely made these countries beneath his notice for now, despite their proximity. Same with the Red Skull, whose schemes over time had grown increasingly personal against Captain America alone. Hydra had their own super-powered agents and always had, dating back to Baron Strucker's attempts at reanimating Nazi corpses. No, using Peristrike Force and Axis Mundi members didn't feel like Hydra at all.

"So, we're more or less agreed that we're proceeding, right?"

"Yes, Congresswoman," Black Widow said giving Cap a sharp, still-disapproving look. He steadily met her gaze.

Ojeda rose and looked down at the red-headed woman. "To the public, a second Avenger on hand is an excellent show of support and of how seriously everyone is taking our security. I know you dislike being in the spotlight, but it helps. And personally, I'll take all the help I can get."

Romanova nodded once and the other woman left the room.

Cap shifted in his chair then winced.

"Steve, we're going into battle in a day or two. How are you feeling, really? Are your fingers healing? Do you want to visit S.H.I.E.L.D.'s sick bay?"

"I'm a fast healer, Natasha. I'll be fine."

"You're also a man who will never admit to weakness. That makes you brave and noble and pretty stupid. Since I am going to be fighting beside you, I need to know how whole you truly are."

"Worried about me fainting during a fight?"

"Don't be flippant, not about your health. Will you be in fighting shape?"

"I'm healing and maybe won't be one hundred percent in two days, but short of the Hulk attacking next, I should be good."

"Famous last words."

* * *

Later that evening, after Ojeda announced to the press they were moving ahead, everyone was invited to a quiet not-quite-reception for just the Americans. Cap suspected it was as much to allow the Slorenians time to mourn their dead and deal with infrastructure issues as much as it was to keep the Americans together for comfort and safety. Being informal, he was able to be out of uniform, which he appreciated, although it exposed some of the bruising on his face, inviting fresh questions from the press, who never seemed to be off duty. The small dining room was nicely appointed with soft music piped in over speakers and an array of hot and cold appetizers on a sideboard. A rolling bar had been brought in with a bartender, the only non-American, on hand.

Simmons and Singer made a beeline for Rogers as soon as he walked into the room wearing an open-collared light-blue button down and chinos.

"You okay, Cap?"

"Fine, thanks," he said.

"Do you feel at all responsible for what happened today?"

"Miss Singer, I was reacting to an attack, how could any of this be my responsibility?"

"You're the symbol of America and that very symbol caused death and destruction. How could you not bear any responsibility?"

"Check your facts. The palace was attacked when I was not there. I responded to an attack and did what I could to ensure the least number of casualties. As always."

"For the record?"

"What are you suggesting, Miss Singer?"

A small crowd of the press had gathered while the delegates kept their distance, none wanting to be drawn into the inquiry. This was supposed to be informal, Rogers reminded himself, but this felt anything but that and he chafed. He had attended as a sign of goodwill and for a chance to unwind, but now he was regretting his choice.

"I am suggesting that American interests seem to be pissing some people off and they're taking it out on our host countries. Do you agree with Ojeda that we should continue rather than go home?"

"My role here is to support the congressional delegation and I will be right beside them. Now, can we please talk about baseball or the movies?"

"Actually, Cap," Simmons said, "I wanted to ask some more about the Russians, the ones from Peristrike Force."

"I'm not done," Singer interrupted. "Clearly, someone wants the Americans gone. Why is the delegation still here? Why are you still here?"

"No, he's done talking shop for the night."

The veteran reporter's head swiveled, followed in the others, as they stared at Natasha Romanova framed in the doorway. She was attired in a stylish green and gold dress that accentuated her curves and muscles. Cap couldn't recall seeing her any more attractive, but he also suspected she did it for effect, to distract the press from seeing her as a super hero or spy. It also drew attention away from him. Once again, she had his back.

He took advantage of the distraction to head farther into the room so he could grab a beer. The bartender flipped off the cap and handed the drink to him with a napkin. He didn't even stop to read the label, just took a long pull to force himself to relax.

"On behalf of journalists around the world, I would like to apologize for her," Amberson said from behind Cap.

"There's got to be one in every pack, right?" Rogers said, tipping the bottle toward the older man in salute.

"I'll take the same," Amberson told the bartender.

The two walked to a window to look out at the city. There were twinkles of light in the sky but below, there were pockets of utter darkness, a result of the day's fighting. It pained Cap to see people suffering for things he was involved in when all he wanted to do was serve people and in this case, that meant protecting them. But since touching down in Europe, there had been death and destruction, and he felt guilty for causing anyone more suffering. It was the dark side of his job, one he didn't like dwelling on, but this trip was making him veer in that direction.

"Ojeda's made a gutsy call," Amberson said. "Going to be interesting to see what happens tomorrow."

"What do you expect?"

"An attack. In fact, I've got Baroness Blood in the pool."

Rogers was surprised at how casual it all felt. Maybe they were being arrogant by proceeding, even inviting an attack. Then again, maybe they should test all the theories and not show up, waiting to see if there was an attack, which would rule out America as a factor. There were so many different ways to look at it, all he knew was they were going, there was going to be an assault of some sort, and he just needed to be ready.

"Put me down for Porcupine Man," he told Amberson. The reporter laughed at that. They were joined by Winters, who was nicely attired in a clinging sweater and tight, wool pants. She was definitely off duty and perhaps on the make.

"He's not in the pool, he's an American. Me, I've got Titanium Man."

"I hope not," Cap said. "That armor hurts."

"Isn't he more an Iron Man enemy?"

"Sure, but in my business, sooner or later you fight everyone."

Winters laughed and shook her head. "I barely remember Titanium Man. Maybe I was still in J-school at the time."

"I would have said diapers," Amberson teased.

"It was a while back," Cap admitted. "He had bulky, green armor. A Russian, so I can see why he made the pool. Who organized it?"

"Gallo," Amberson said, gesturing toward the congressional aide.

"Seriously, Cap . . ." Winters began before he corrected her.

"I'm off duty, call me Steve."

"Seriously, Steve, aren't you worried about tomorrow?" She hesitated a moment and then, placing her hand on his forearm, "Off the record. The whole night is off the record."

Maybe he was being overly sensitive, but he suspected there was more to her statement than just her initial question.

"Worried? No, not really. Wary? Of course. We all anticipate an attack but by whom or when is going to be preoccupying us and the Carnelians. Tomorrow, in some ways, is going to be our most challenging day yet, simply because we'll be on alert 24/7."

"You really need to relax then," she said, handing him another beer and offering a smile that was pleasant and certainly inviting.

Cap opened his mouth to mention Sharon, but before he could, Amberson swooped in to rescue the increasingly awkward moment. "Norah, let's let the good captain enjoy his peace before tomorrow." He steered her toward Brenda Swanson who, as usual, was quiet and leaning against the wall. She certainly looked more in need of companionship than he did.

"In my book, we call that a save," Al Jackson said with a grin.

"Yeah," Rogers said and took a drink.

"Sweet kid, but she's got stars in her eyes."

"We were young once, too, right?"

"Sure. Me, I was playing A-ball throughout the south before getting called up to the bigs. Made my debut at twenty and had a pretty good run."

"Sorry I never saw you pitch."

"You were otherwise occupied, if I recall," Jackson said, referring to the years of suspended animation that had prolonged Captain America's life while distancing him from friends and family in unimaginable ways.

"Congress any better?"

"After I retired I could have stuck around and coached, but by then, my interests were different. Traveling meant I got to see some really great places, but even more that needed help. I figured it was time pay it back, do something about it."

"How long have you been in Congress?"

"It's my fifth term, probably sticking around a bit more."

"Thinking about the Senate at all?"

Jackson chuckled and said, "Now you're sounding like them." At Rogers' surprised reaction he smiled again and added, "It's fine, I get it all the time. I've invested ten years in the House and forged some good ties across the aisle. My seniority is getting good, too, so I'm getting better committees. So, do I trade all that for something different? Choices and consequences."

"Like tomorrow," Cap said, unable to keep the concern from his voice.

"Yeah, like tomorrow. You want a scouting report on the opponent, but it's all a big mystery. Better make sure that shield is nicely polished."

The men continued to speak throughout the evening, but the following day's threats were never far from Rogers' mind. Occasionally, he would look across the room and see Black Widow chatting quietly, avoiding the press wherever possible, sticking with Seaver and Martinez while Ojeda bounced between the press and her fellow members of Congress. Black Widow was clearly sizing up all the players, seeking clues in case there was a traitor somewhere in their midst. While he never articulated it, he had to consider whether or not there was some mole in their traveling group; nothing had appeared to him, but she had the better training for finding secrets. Her body language betrayed nothing, so if she'd found something, he'd learn about it later.

Given their early departure, the evening wound down at a reasonable hour with the congresswoman making a final round of the press corps and ushering them out of the room. After tipping the waiter, it was just the delegation, Black Widow, and Cap.

"We all know tomorrow's going to be a rough one, so get some sleep and be ready for anything," Ojeda told them. "We've got the best protection you could ask for, but we still have no idea from who or what or when."

With that somber thought lingering in the air, everyone made their good nights and left for their rooms.

Steve Rogers could operate on few hours of sleep but given his injuries, he needed more time to let his body heal. Still, lying alone in bed, he had trouble draining what ifs from his mind until the early hours, when sleep finally claimed him.

CHAPTER SIX

It was clear to Steve Rogers that everyone was feeling tense as they boarded the plane for the trip to Carnelia. His body still felt sore and he would not have said no to a massage or an extra day for his fingers, but he was given little say in the flight schedule. The bright sun and crisp spring air did not lighten anyone's spirits as the sense of foreboding outweighed the anticipation of seeing the final country on the itinerary. Instead, like everyone else in the delegation and press corps, Rogers knew there would be an attack, so he boarded in uniform rather than civilian gear. The gallows humor of the betting pool may have cut the tension the previous evening, but now that they were flying toward certain danger, no one was joking.

The press continued to ask the four delegates about the wisdom of heading toward a country that was going to be attacked in some way. The best Roberta Ojeda could do was say that if there was an attack against the Carnelian people, the Americans would bear witness and stand by their allies.

Although, ally might be too optimistic a word to use with the country. It wasn't all that long ago that Carnelia faced global condemnation over their fusion reactor facility, which was thankfully exposed and dismantled by the Thunderbolts. This brought about the ousting of Prime Minister Nikolas Kitsenko and election of the better-loved Nina Sergeevna Krilova.

As the plane cruised into Carnelian airspace, it was immediately flanked by twin jets from the small country's air force. There was an almost audible sigh of relief from the press as the escort arrived, which brought a small smile to Rogers. It instantly faded when he saw the look on Natasha Romanova's face, her fingers cupping her right ear. With diminishing patience, he waited for her to complete receiving the message and waited for the bad news.

"The *Crescent* has been attacked. Warrior Woman and Scattershot got out," she told him.

"How?"

"They're trying to figure it out. Something about an attack as they were being prepared for transport."

"Transport? On whose orders? Never mind, when did this happen? Where are they?"

"About two hundred miles behind us and about ten minutes ago. It's pretty garbled because they're trying to avoid crash landing anywhere in Europe. We were being warned."

"Because they're coming after us," he finished.

"Most likely."

The plane and their escort dipped their noses, preparing to land, and Captain America's mind raced through scenarios.

"Neither of them can fly, so I presume they stole something they can fly faster than this plane."

As if to confirm his comment, a bright-yellow bolt reflected through his window and in horror, he watched as a Carnelian jet was blown apart. The attack was so sudden that the pilot had no time to eject and was lost along with the craft, the remains of which dropped from the sky. Black Widow was already out of her seat and moving toward the cockpit when a second searing shot took out the other air force jet.

Cap rose, unstrapped the shield from the seat beside him, slipped his arm through the straps and tightened his grip, wincing as his cracked left hand tried to get a comfortable grip on the strap.

Screams and questions made talking difficult as panic swept through the airplane, as everyone except Captain America, who knew Julia Koenig would never go for the quick kill (she wanted to make him suffer), was convinced they were next. He wanted to offer comfort but it was time for action. They'd fought one another in two different eras, and despite her great tactical knowledge, she could be predictable. What was unpredictable was all the debris hitting the airplane. A giant piece of the jet plane smashed into the front of the airliner, and he heard the sickening rip of metal. Luckily, the air pressure didn't change, so nothing was punctured, but he feared for the engines.

The plane dove at a frightening angle, tossing the unbuckled from their seats; tablets, laptops, books, and drinks flew around the cabin. Black Widow pounded against the secure door. When there was no reply, she adjusted her wrist blaster and fired off a sting that shattered the locking mechanism. Quickly, she entered the cockpit and a black-gloved hand immediately reappeared with a gesture summoning her partner.

Moving without tumbling out of control was challenging as Cap gripped each seat and worked his way forward, row by row, until he reached the door. Romanova stuck her head out to say, "Both pilots are injured. We're in a dive and I have to fly the plane. You have to stop them."

She closed the door and within seconds the craft leveled out, a few degrees at a time. Cap, though, couldn't appreciate her deft control as he had to focus on the attackers in a S.H.I.E.L.D. air transport, a Hoverflier, which was far more maneuverable than a 767 heavy cruiser. The opposing craft was wide and flat nosed, normally built for just two, and with two deadly cannons mounted beneath. As far as he could tell, it was pacing the plane, which gave him an opportunity.

Avoiding questions and pleas from the various passengers, Cap accessed a panel at the rear of the plane, allowing him to reach the luggage storage. Thankfully, it was tightly packed and tied down, giving him the freedom to get to an emergency hatch and ensuring nothing moved when he popped the hatch and the air rushed out. He ignored the roaring, rushing sound of air that assaulted his hearing in the hold. Instead, holding tight to several straps, he studied the sight below him, wisps of clouds and then the glint of metal. He saw the Hoverflier, calculated speed and distance, then counted down from five, slipped the shield over his shoulders, and leapt.

He'd jumped from planes before, with and without a parachute, and was accustomed to the sudden rush of air tugging at his body. As gently as possible, he angled himself so he now sped toward the Hoverflier, closing the distance in seconds. At the last moment, he twisted and made contact against the short wing, his added weight forcing the vehicle to dip. He scrambled for purchase and held on, counting on his sore muscles to keep him in place. Hand over hand, he painfully inched to the main body of the stolen flier until he could peer in a window.

Scattershot's masked face sneered at him, cursing, although he couldn't make out the words.

Koenig was piloting and put the Hoverflier through its paces in an attempt to shake Cap free. After three or four attempts, she seemed resigned to his being a human barnacle. Scattershot couldn't fire at him without depressurizing the craft, but the cannon could still take out the American airplane, so Cap knew he had to act. He inched forward and spread-eagled himself over the yellow S.H.I.E.L.D. symbol, staring directly at his old opponent. Risking losing his grip, he lifted his right glove and pointed with his index finger that the Hoverflier should land.

Warrior Woman's acknowledgment used a different finger.

She rolled the flier and Captain America nearly lost his grasp, then she rolled a second and a third time. He continued to hold on and when she righted the Hoverflier, he pointed to the ground again.

All the while, he noticed that Black Widow continued the American plane's descent and had even managed to angle it away from the Hoverflier. If anything, he was distracting the women and keeping the other plane out of the line of fire. Still, he now had to focus on his next steps. If Koenig wouldn't land voluntarily, he would have to force her down.

Carefully, he shrugged the shield from his shoulders and then, taking a risk, tossed it into the air. The wind pushed it farther away than he anticipated, but it curved as expected and came toward the flier. Then, with a fierce clang, it bit into the tail, nearly slicing into a good two feet of metal, and wedged in place. The shield did its job, making the plane wobble unsteadily in the air.

To compound matters, Cap balled his left hand into a fist and smashed it against the windshield. It took just one punch to crack the reinforced glass. Koenig's eyes went wide and Cap could see Scattershot's hands heat up as Warrior Woman snapped at her not to exacerbate things. Cap reared back and struck again, creating a web of cracks.

Both he and the pilot knew a third blow would shatter the window, causing them to lose pressure and control of the already-damaged flier. Koenig, to her credit, gestured she was landing the stolen craft. Only then did Cap risk a look over his shoulder to see Carnelia's sole international airport looming large beneath them. In the distance, the compromised 767 was nearing touchdown, so he could focus entirely on the women.

Julia Koenig was not going to make this easy—she shook and wobbled the damaged craft, trying to force Captain America off or at least rattle him. It worked—he felt additional pressure along his torso and legs but never once let go. The cracked fingers on his left hand struggled to stay in place and the pain was growing. Using the Hoverflier's VTOL capabilities, she brought it straight down and landed hard, one final insult to her opponent.

It was then that Scattershot let loose a red-hot beam of pure energy that shattered the glass and singed the air over Cap's head. Knowing he had twenty seconds before she could fire again, he scrambled up and over the tiny cockpit to retrieve his shield. As he cleared the ruined cockpit, Warrior Woman's black glove reached through the torn metal and broken glass to grab his boot. With a savage tug, she pulled him back, trying to get a good grip to break his leg.

Instead, he delivered a fierce kick with his other boot and, holding on to the roof, yanked his feet free. Seconds later, he was able to extract his weapon and slip it back into place in his left hand.

With a snarl, Koenig burst through the aperture and leapt to the tarmac. "Well played, Captain! Now, you will finally suffer, dying away from your precious country."

She leapt up at him, her powerful legs propelling her with the speed of a missile but Captain America braced himself and held his shield before him. The impact was jaw shattering but he gritted his teeth and let the force push him back and over the Hoverflier's roof. He did a backflip and neatly landed on the ground. Warrior Woman sailed over the craft as well, going into a forward roll then springing to her feet, poised to fight.

Behind him, Cap heard the renewed crackle of plasma being generated by Scattershot. With a flick of his hand, he sent the shield toward her, letting the sound of it impacting against her and her shriek of pain tell him she would not be a problem for now. He planted his feet in position and his body tensed to wrestle Koenig. She had pulled out her whip and it cracked loudly in the air as its end wrapped around his right wrist. Then, she tugged and he was hefted off his feet, an unwilling object in the air. Reeling him in, Warrior Woman dropped the whip and put him in a crushing bear hug, squeezing the air from his chest.

Scattershot, meanwhile, finally clambered from the crippled flier and reached the ground. The air sizzled before her and she curled her lip. "This is going to hurt."

"Do it!" commanded Warrior Woman.

Scattershot unleashed the blast at the very moment Cap folded forward, pulling Warrior Woman directly into the line of fire. The impact staggered even someone with reinforced skin and musculature. Cap broke free and delivered a two-handed blow to the woman's jaw before dashing for Scattershot. There was enough time for him to close the distance between them before she could fire again. She was not physically enhanced and crumpled with the first punch.

He let her drop to the tarmac then retrieved his shield just as Warrior Woman recovered and bellowed, a painful sound Cap did not want to hear a second time. Enraged, she rushed him and they traded punches with ferocity. There was no elegance to her attack, no art to the fight, just rage.

Rogers ducked and twisted, his more agile body able to miss or deflect most of the blows. In turn, he weakened her softer midsection with his fists. Ideally, he'd be able to reach one of her nerve clusters and seriously incapacitate her, but she was fast and the constant motion prevented that strategy. Cap also recognized it was only a matter of time before Scattershot rejoined the battle.

With a flip, he avoided another roundhouse punch and struck back with the face of his shield, sending Warrior Woman backward. She was bleeding from several cuts and her hair was coming loose from its tightly coiled braid. She was finally starting to breathe heavily, proving that even a product of Germany super science had her limits.

Behind him, he heard several sounds coming from different directions: the now-familiar buildup of Scattershot's plasma energy and that of a truck. He dared to look away from Koenig to survey the scene, making certain civilians were nowhere near them.

Scattershot shouted something in Russian and he could only imagine what she was saying. She unleashed twin bursts of raw, white-hot plasma directly at Cap and he wondered how much of the blast his shield could deflect and how much might still burn him. Then he heard Warrior Woman running toward him, intending to hold him in place to take the brunt of the blast.

Instead, Koenig flew forward as a fuel truck rammed into her from behind. Its driver, Black Widow, dove from the cabin, tumbling into a graceful roll in the opposite direction, away from the blast.

Cap dropped to the ground as the plasma burst sailed over him, but the chain mail conducted much of the vicious heat, burning him. Warrior Woman was also missed by the plasma burst, as she was struggling to regain her footing. The blasts, though, hit the truck instead of the humans, and there was an ear-splitting explosion and a ball of flame flared brightly, rendering the German stunned, if not unconscious.

Aching, Cap rose to his knees to see the conflagration. The fire seemed contained to a tight circle around where the truck impacted with Warrior Woman. Her leather outfit was on fire, adhering to her blistering skin, much of which remained exposed to the flames, which were lapping at her from head to toe. It hurt to move, but he forced himself toward the heat and, using the shield to protect him, he neared the unconscious woman. He grabbed her wrist with his right hand and dragged her away from the flames until the air felt cooler.

Sirens filled the air and in the distance, two fire engines raced in his direction. He looked at the scene, suddenly realizing he had never secured Scattershot and scanned for her. His eyes focused on Black Widow standing over the downed red-and-black-clad woman, also unconscious. Romanova was already on her comm link to S.H.I.E.L.D., no doubt ordering some backup with proper restraints.

"You okay?"

"I'm banged up and a bit burned," Cap told her. "The congressmen?"

"Rattled but whole. Everyone's in a hangar until we give them the all clear."

"What happened on the *Crescent*? Are Phillips and the others alive?"

"A few casualties and lots of collateral damage."

Cap nodded in acknowledgment then gestured toward Koenig. "She's in bad shape and will need a burn unit. Some welcome we're giving the government."

"You saved the Americans, stopped dangerous super-powered enemies, and kept it all away from the citizenry. All in all, I think the PM will be happy with your performance. Do *you* need a burn unit?"

"A ton of aloe, I think. Natasha, this was something new, a wild card."

"I know. They got free somehow and that wasn't the plan."

"Someone else is still gunning for the prime minister. We have to get to Pershyy Misto."

"You're in no shape to fight, Steve," she said gently.

"No choice, Natasha," he said.

The fire engines had arrived and the crew were already hosing down the fuel truck's remains and the surrounding tarmac. Warrior Woman's inert form was also soaked, allowing a paramedic team to begin treating her.

"What do we do with Scattershot? She'll wake up and recharge all over again," Cap asked.

"I've put a call in and reinforcements are coming for her. I can stay and keep watch. Go get treated before the real attack happens."

He grunted and slowly walked toward the EMTs; every step hurt as the uniform chafed against burned or bruised skin. Thankfully, English was spoken well enough here that he could make his issues understood. Gingerly, he peeled off the top of his uniform and a gruff older man made tsk-tsk noises as he examined Cap's battered body. Quickly, the paramedic dabbed an ointment over the burned spots and applied topical first-aid cream to the hero's cuts. While Rogers healed quickly and could endure a lot, the last few days had really worn him down and he hoped, after the attack du jour was dealt with, the fighting would stop today. Of course, that still left the mastermind, along with the all-important *why,* behind all this in the shadows.

Scattershot stirred while the EMT worked on Cap. He saw Black Widow calmly zap her once more, leaving Scattershot too groggy to actually power up and cause damage. Finally, two Hoverfliers came in low and fast, heading directly toward the remains of the wreckage. With quiet efficiency, four agents exited the craft and applied energy dampeners to Scattershot's hands, then trussed her up for transport.

As they worked, Cap ambled over to them, exchanging nods. "What's the Helicarrier status?"

"Limping badly and heading for repairs. After we take these two into custody, we're bugging out of Europe."

"How'd this happen?" Black Widow demanded.

"We have no clue, but it's being investigated."

"We want updates," she insisted. The agent nodded once then addressed himself to figuring out how best to transport the badly burned, still-unconscious Warrior Woman. As they worked, Captain America and Black Widow walked slowly toward the hangar and the rest of their party. Neither said a word, but no doubt she was figuring out how to handle a fight with a wounded Star-Spangled Avenger, while he focused more on how best to protect the prime minister, who would be the target if the pattern continued.

A fleet of black SUVs paraded into the airport and headed for the hangar. One peeled off and headed for the costumed heroes. A man in military uniform popped from the passenger side and held open the door, gesturing for them to enter. Black Widow went first and Cap followed, noticing how something as simple as climbing into a car hurt. She handed him a bottle of water, which he guzzled down in record time. Drinking the second bottle more slowly, he allowed himself to relax as he watched the Hoverfliers rise up simultaneously and zoom out of sight.

At least Julia Koenig would get the treatment she needed, but it also meant S.H.I.E.L.D. could no longer lend logistical support for the time being. Whoever was coming next would become a local containment problem, and he doubted the small country, with just three million residents, had the necessary facilities.

The driver and military passenger said nothing as they

resumed their place in the formation. Once the Americans were boarded, the fleet of SUVs raced from the airport and toward Pershyy Misto's House of Parliament, where the meeting was scheduled. Cap figured he had time to refocus his thoughts, but the rolling hills at the base of the Carpathian Mountains lulled him and soon he closed his eyes.

When he opened them, the cars were rolling to a stop before the tall, colorful House, which was built along Russian Imperial architectural style, which made sense since the land was once under Soviet control until it broke away in the 1920s. By the time he felt ready to leave his SUV, the delegates were already being escorted into the building, Black Widow at their side. The press corps were shouting questions from ten feet back and were ignored. They were, though, joined by local media, so their ranks had swelled. All Cap saw were more targets to protect.

He stood beside the SUV and assessed himself. The ointment and cream seemed to tame the worst of his pain but he ached and his ribs remained tender. His uniform was blackened and torn in spots, his gleaming shield the sole exception. Ideally, he'd like a soaking bath, a massage, a steak, and eight hours' sleep, but instead, the mission demanded he remain alert for now.

The attack was coming. He was sure of it.

Once everyone was inside the House, Cap strode forward, projecting his military bearing, faking confidence. The structure was almost as impressive from the inside as it was from the outside, with old handcraftsmanship evident on the columns and ornate archways. The marble busts of previous prime ministers were nestled in cylindrical alcoves, each bearing a plaque with the names and years of service. Cap noticed the ornate tapestries and paintings that filled up the walls, and he overheard the general buzz of conversation in the air. Many Carnelians paused to watch Cap pass, snapping pictures with their cell phones. If anyone was monitoring the situation, social media made certain to announce his presence in the seat of government.

The building had large chambers for the members but he was escorted toward a meeting room adjacent to the prime minister's office. He could hear Jackson's voice telling the story to someone. The very normalcy of tone reassured him the Americans were calmly handling the situation. Black Widow stood near the doorway, and they exchanged looks. He understood that she'd checked the room and everything seemed clear.

Prime Minister Krilova was small, maybe a few inches above five feet, trim, and seemingly young, midthirties at the latest. She had a dark complexion, black hair, and a winning smile, which she flashed at Ojeda. They were side by side, posing for the press while the three congressmen spoke with cabinet officials.

Everything seemed so normal; no one betrayed the mounting pressure that everyone felt. Cap ascribed it to his arriving after things got started and the prime minister's desire to keep matters free of drama. Overhead, Cap heard the jets patrolling the skies over the capital city, which was somewhat reassuring. Still, without knowing who was coming, when, or how, security was an illusion of wishful thinking.

"We have much to offer America," Krilova was saying in response to a question. "Our metal ores alone would be wanted by Silicon Valley."

"Have you and America kissed and made up?" Singer asked, earning her disapproving looks from the other Americans.

"If you're referring to the murder of Ambassador Kotznin, that is old business. It was unfortunate and beyond Iron Man's control. Apologies and reparations have been made," Krilova said stiffly. It was Justin Hammer, Tony Stark's rival, who hacked into the Iron Man armor and killed the UN ambassador, almost igniting a war between the two countries. It helped Stark along the path to alcoholism, Cap recalled, and then shoved the memory away.

"You're open to doing business, then, with the United States?" Amberson continued.

"I would not have invited the delegation here if it were otherwise," Krilova replied, flashing her smile at Ojeda.

A rumble from outside instantly raised the hair on the back of Cap's neck. Black Widow strode toward a window to get a visual. Everyone flinched as much from the heroes swinging into action as from the increasingly loud mechanical sound.

Captain America turned to the solider at his right and snapped, "Get everyone in this room to the most secure place in the building. Lock it down until I personally give you the all clear. Understood."

"*Da.* . . . Y-y-yes," he stammered in reply. Then he waved his hand in the air, signaling everyone to follow him.

Captain America and Black Widow rushed from the room, down the marble corridor, and onto the street. Jets roared overhead and they saw nothing else in the sky, so they concentrated on the streets leading to Parliament. Cars raced down one street, stampeding out of the way of something red and bulky coming their way.

"Who is that?"

"I don't recognize him," Black Widow replied. "What does that say about the opponents when we can't even make an ID?"

"It means they are either new or low-level threats. Similar to Psi-Wolf and . . ." His words were cut off when the red-armored figure scooped up a small panel truck and threw it ahead of him. The truck folded up as it struck the pavement and a parked car. People ran in every direction away from the figure and as it neared Parliament, Cap spotted the golden hammer and sickle painted on the armor's chest plating. Another Russian foe, one reason he couldn't immediately recognize him . . . or her.

As it stalked closer, Cap analyzed the armor and its movements, calculating points of attack. It was large and bulky, but rounded and streamlined. The arms nearly reached the street and the helmet was small and squat, making the rest of the body appear out of proportion. Various protuberances along the neck and shoulders indicated they contained something; perhaps weapons, gases, or just oxygen. He cursed himself for feeling unprepared but reminded himself there were so many threats that there was no way he could keep track of them all.

"An android or robot?"

"I don't think so. The gait is too uneven, too human to be programmed," Cap observed.

"It's all brawn," Black Widow noted.

"No offensive weaponry, then," Cap said. "No energy blasts or projectiles."

"But defensive armor plating," she added. To illustrate the point, sharpshooters from the second floor above them opened fire as it entered range. Bullets struck the figure with high-pitched clangs but the impact didn't slow its progress toward Parliament. It did not fire back, which also confirmed Cap's suspicions about weapons.

The armor alone would make an attack difficult, but not impossible. Cap rejected numerous strategies as the armored figure's capabilities came into focus. His super-soldier-derived strength and his shield would have to do. His muscles ached and he was battered all over, so this was not going to be a fun fight. With luck, he could expose the human within and knock him out. Trucks carrying the Carnelian army roared into view and men poured out. A commanding officer spotted Captain America and tossed a hasty salute his way.

"Get the people clear, then form a perimeter around Parliament!" Captain America ordered and then sprinted toward the figure without waiting for confirmation. He didn't wait for acknowledgment or pause to apologize for usurping the chain of command—time was short. By putting himself between the army and the armor, he hoped this enemy would not immediately open fire. Rapid foot slaps behind him confirmed Black Widow followed his lead.

Cap neared the large figure and hurled his shield while simultaneously leaping onto a car's hood and propelling himself at the metallic head. The red and white weapon slammed into the form but did little beyond chipping away some of the paint. He was more successful, straddling the head and staring directly at the T-shaped view screen.

Black Widow, in a well-practiced move, grabbed the falling shield and tossed it up to Cap, who grabbed it and smashed it into the seam where the helmet was welded to the torso. The sharp edge cut into the metal without truly splitting it apart. The armored form, for its part, reached up and grabbed Cap with both hands and yanked him from its head. The arms tossed him across the street and it began to stalk Black Widow.

Smashing into the car set off the alarm and made Cap see spots. Shaking off the pain, he stood and reassessed the armored figure.

"This walking flag moves slowly," he said.

"That's it," she called from the opposite side of the street where she stood atop a car's roof, dancing to the next one over to avoid being grabbed. "He's called Red Flag!"

"Really? Are they running out of names?"

"He's some scientist who built the armor and now uses it to fund his research or something. There's a kid involved, too," she said.

The information made Cap reassess how to attack an enemy who was all brains yet not an experienced fighter. It explained a lot of why it was merely walking toward Parliament. "Stay with me," he called and once more leapt at the armored scientist. He grabbed onto the large buttons at the base of the neck and once more slammed his shield into the small rip he'd made in the armor. This time, there was a sound of shrieking metal ripping apart and a hole formed.

"Now!" he called as he flipped from the armored form,

avoided being grabbed, and landed with jarring impact on the street.

Black Widow took aim and fired her sting once but missed the exposed circuitry. She would have to get closer. She hopped from car to car, then did an acrobatic flip to land on its back. She reached around its neck and fired point blank into the torn metal, flooding the works with electric charges. Smoke steamed out and she could hear overloads blowing out fuses and relays.

Pushing herself off its back, she floated through the air, twisted, turned, and landed on both feet, ready for the next step.

Black smoke streamed from the armor as the arms flailed and obscured the now-cracked faceplates. Red Flag tried to turn toward Black Widow but something snapped, then popped, and one arm refused to move. A stream of Russian curses came from a speaker—Cap couldn't understand it, but the tone was different from anger.

"He's carrying a plague toxin in the armor and he's afraid we'll unleash it," Black Widow translated.

It made sense a scientist would devise a chemical weapon of some sort, but to walk around with it was reckless. Cap realized that must have been the plan all along, to poison not just the prime minister but all of Parliament and maybe the American delegation, too.

He cursed himself for not having direct contact with

Ojeda or the ability to summon the army. They had to contain the armor in case its occupant was right. As he considered options, Black Widow approached the frozen form and spoke to it. She probed the large buttons, which seemed to contain the toxin, and made certain they were affixed.

"We may have caught a break," she called and Cap carefully joined her.

"Everything is secure and he thinks they won't be released. But he's also trapped and will have to be cut out of there. It seems he's been working merely to maintain the armor since it's expensive. He's using outdated tech and frankly, is in way over his head."

"Did he say who hired him?"

"Anonymous from the dark web, wired payment—the usual."

The two wearily returned to the parliament building and were escorted into the conference room as the prime minister and the Americans were just getting settled now that Cap had given the all clear. Krilova did not look happy; in fact, she was radiating displeasure.

"Can you explain this? You warned us there would be an attack, but today there were *two*. There is careless disregard for our airspace, our borders. Not long ago, your Thunderbolts entered our sovereign space and attacked one of our facilities. Just how much do our borders mean to the likes of you and your American masters?"

"I have no American master," Romanova said bluntly.

She was about to say more when Cap spoke over her. "Madame Prime Minister, you were warned that your country was likely to be attacked. We did that out of concern and friendship. The attack at the airport is connected but not something we anticipated. That was a failing with S.H.I.E.L.D., which I remind you is an international, not American, peacekeeping organization."

"They do a very poor job of it," Krilova spat. "I will expect reparations for the airport damage—from America or S.H.I.E.L.D., I do not care. But understand something, it took us some time to recover from the biomodem brainwashing that afflicted my people. Then our treaty with Trebekistan was interfered with by ULTIMATUM . . ."

"And was stopped by the Avengers," Captain America reminded her.

"Yes, because the prime minister at the time was threatened in New York," she shot back. "We seem to be a pawn in someone else's grand scheme . . . again. Our sovereign desires seem not to matter to anyone and that must change. We may be small, but we still are an independent nation, and should be respected as much."

Ojeda had neared the conversation and finally interjected herself, coming into Krilova's view and distracting the smaller woman. "That's why we're here, Madame Prime Minister. We would like to talk about better relations and yes, better respect. Earlier you mentioned your ores; why don't we start there?"

Gently, Ojeda steered the woman away from the heroes and toward the congressmen and Carnelians. It was a deft performance that Cap had to admire.

"She's a feisty one," Black Widow said in a whisper.

"Can you really blame her?"

She shook her head.

"While they negotiate, call Sharon. Something's wrong. Scattershot and Koenig never should have been moved."

"I'm on it."

NOVEMBER 11, 1944

"Another death-ray cannon, are you serious?"

Bucky and Captain America were trudging through the Tumi Pass in the Western Carpathian Mountains, searching for Baron Heinrich Zemo, the brilliant but deadly Nazi scientist. The trio had clashed numerous times in the past, but the wily German always seemed to elude capture, which explained why the two were seeking him just over the Carnelian border. The tiny country had been used to bring supplies across the battlefront but was largely spared the fighting and bombing.

"I hope you have your passport handy, Bucky, you've now entered Carnelia," Cap cracked.

"How do you keep them all straight? These names tie up my tongue and I always seem to be getting them confused. Slorenia, Slovakia, Symkaria, Sweden, Switzerland—are they hung up on the letter *S*?"

"I study the maps, something you should be doing more of," Cap chided him.

The transport had left them at the base of the path in Slovakia and now, several miles later, they were in another country. Somewhere in this pass, though, were a series of caverns where Zemo was thought to be testing his latest version of the powerful death ray, a particle-energy weapon that instantaneously killed its targets. Cap, Bucky, and the Howling Commandos had taken out the first such creation, but Zemo had been continuing his work, having first miniaturized it into a pistol. Who knew what he was doing with it now.

Zemo had grown increasingly dangerous, having recently killed Citizen V with his bare hands in Poland. Now he was back to building weapons that would embolden the Nazi army.

"Okay, Mr. Geography, why here?"

"The Western Carpathian Mountains are rich in iron, silver, and gold. I suspect he needs one or more of those ores. It's also fairly remote and difficult to access," Cap said. "And that's Captain Geography," he finished with a grin.

"That explains why they sent us," Bucky said, wrapping himself tighter in the heavy olive-green parka he had been assigned. The temperatures were dropping as winter settled over Eastern Europe. Cap had hoped the war might be over by now, but no, 1944 was ending without a real sense of when the campaign would end with an Allied victory. Stopping Zemo would certainly hasten that.

Over the last few years, he'd watched friends be maimed

or killed, and he'd totally lost contact with Sgt. Duffy and his company. Even the tough-to-kill Nick Fury had taken shrapnel to one eye and was losing sight in it. Not that it stopped Rogers, but even the toughest soldiers were getting worn down by the fighting. And once Hitler was stopped, there was still Hideki Tojo to deal with in the Pacific.

Christmas was looming, and he was thinking about going home, seeing what sort of life Steve Rogers could have. If Peggy Carter was going to stay in Europe, he might remain, or maybe follow her back to the States. Could they still love one another without bullets whizzing overhead?

Even Bucky, no longer a kid, was talking about life after the war. On their last leave, he had met Francesca, a displaced French teen. She was pretty and sassy, and although they'd known each other just three days, Cap could tell Bucky had fallen for her—hard.

Images of home warmed Cap and he was humming "I'll be Home for Christmas" when the first bullet chipped rock over his head.

Instantly, shield before him, Captain America pushed thoughts of home from his mind. The soldier was ready for combat.

Guards had to be stationed around the bend, meaning they were nearing Zemo's lair. They heard running footsteps, reinforcements. Bucky took up position behind Cap, rifle at the ready.

Cap looked around and realized there were few options,

and none of them great. He heard Bucky scrambling on stone and realized his partner had shucked off the coat—his red and blue uniform clearly visible—and was clambering up the side of the mountain, seeking a vantage point from which to provide cover.

Cap crouched and moved forward, letting the shield deflect the bullets. If that was the worst they had, he could deal with it. He feared, though, some new, fantastic weapon. He had to hand it to Zemo, Arnim Zola, Wolfgang Strucker, and Doctor Kraus—they devised things Cap could never have imagined. Thankfully, for every menace they created, America and its allies countered them, hero for villain, weapon for weapon. When this was over, the world would be a very different one.

The staccato rhythm of machine-gun fire hit his shield, forcing him to slow down, but he remained unyielding. Nor did he look up once to give away his partner's gambit. Instead, he focused on the men before him, four in all, dressed in the long, green coats the army wore. One was bareheaded, the others wore woolen caps, all looking in need of a shave and hot meal. The four fired simultaneously and while the shield deflected the bullets, the ricochets were causing rocks to splinter and natural shrapnel stung him. He dared to glance up and noticed Bucky giving him a thumbs-up, then taking aim from his perch above.

The German with the machine gun fell over, the air quickly growing silent.

The other three looked around, then finally one looked up, and as he lifted his own rifle, Bucky fired once.

Taking advantage of the distraction, Cap sprang forward, letting his fists take out the other two, leaving them in a stunned heap. He checked the pulses of the two who were shot to make certain they were dead, but he knew Bucky had become an expert marksman as a result of all his recent field experience.

No doubt, the shots warned Zemo, so rather than wait for Bucky to reach the ground, Cap sprinted forward to the cavern with electric lights and a small generator powering them by the entrance. Cautiously, he peered within the cave and saw the remains of mining and electronics and shattered vacuum tubes mixed in with sifted rock, forming heaps on a side table.

There was no sign of Zemo. It was possible he was long gone.

As long as Zemo remained active, the war would never end. But Cap felt the pull of home more strongly than any magnetic force he had encountered. The Nazi surrender could not come quickly enough.

CHAPTER SEVEN

As Captain America and Black Widow entered the corridor, several members of the press followed them, trailed by Gallo, the congressional assistant. With a heavy sigh, Cap knew he would have to face questions from the press when what he wanted were answers.

Sure enough, the first assault came from Singer, "Do you have any response to Krilova's accusation?"

"As I told her inside, we respect their borders and are here to defend them. We didn't invite Scattershot or Warrior Woman to attack."

She followed up, "Isn't your very presence a provocation?"

"We were simply accepting an invitation."

"Shouldn't we have canceled the trip, knowing our presence was putting Carnelian lives at risk?"

"Actually, Miss Singer, you will note that the attacks were not directed at any American before now."

"So, why the attacks at all?" Norah Winters asked.

"That's under investigation. It's as much a mystery to us as it is to you."

Winters continued, "What does it say that two super-powered women could escape S.H.I.E.L.D.? Are they less effective than they used to be?"

Cap winced. The espionage and law-enforcement agency had taken its lumps over the years. For every victory they achieved, the agency seemed to flub something else. Compromising a Helicarrier was a black spot and a budgetary strain at a time few countries were supporting their massive financial needs. He was just thankful he had Sharon Carter overseeing the operation from the central command Helicarrier back in America.

"S.H.I.E.L.D. remains the world's first line of defense against global threats, never lose sight of that. Given the size and scope of those threats, there will be damage and consequences, but overall, we remain stronger with them in action."

"Who was that outside?"

"He is a Russian scientist who goes by the code name Red Flag," Cap said.

"They're running out of good names," Amberson quipped.

"Maybe."

"What happened to him?"

"Black Widow incapacitated the armor's electronics and Red Flag is immobilized outside, surrounded by guards, and awaiting arrest."

There was a squeaky sound behind them and the press turned toward Gallo, who, with an impish grin, said, "Oil can!"

Chuckles cut through the tension, allowing Cap to complete the impromptu press conference without further barbed questioning. When he felt he had done his duty, he thanked the reporters and spun on his heel, heading for the doors.

Once he and Black Widow hit the street, they saw not only a squad of soldiers surrounding the frozen figure of Red Flag, but also a tank in position. He considered it overkill but wasn't about to tell the Carnelian army how to do their job. The pair walked near Red Flag and saw that nothing had changed and he posed no further threat.

A well-pressed officer walked over to them and saluted. "I am Captain Hordiyenko and the prime minister has asked that we escort you as you tour our city."

"That's really not necessary," Cap began but saw the apologetic look in the man's eyes. "Prime minister's orders?"

The captain continued to smile placidly.

"Which way shall we go, then?"

"I would recommend east, toward our memorials," the captain suggested, holding out an arm in an "after you" gesture.

Four soldiers accompanied Captain America and Black Widow, with Amberson, Winters, and Singer following along, surveying the damage Red Flag had inflicted.

The nine men and women walked down one street, shoppers and passersby pausing to gape or record the moment. Walking felt good despite Cap's aches and pains—if he couldn't get a hot bath, movement would have to do. The European architecture was fairly generic, at least to his practiced eye. The buildings rarely topped five or six stories, most clearly having been erected decades earlier. There was a mixture of typical shops topped by apartments, light traffic, and the smell of frying onions competing with the nearby bakery. Rogers realized it had been some time since he had eaten and would have to remedy that soon. Sadly, there were no curbside food trucks or hot-dog vendors in sight. Then again, he didn't have any local currency on hand.

Instead, the group walked largely in silence as they visited the city. Clearly, Captain Hordiyenko knew the territory, nodding at people he recognized, pausing to shake a few hands. They headed straight for several blocks then made a right turn into a lush-looking park. It was a semicircle of greenery and budding flowers in a spray of white, orange, and yellow. There were two expertly carved statues made from granite, marble, and bronze. The one to the left was a helmet atop a bayonet, with other rifles scattered around it in a frozen tableau of the First World War's no man's land.

The other piece of artwork was far more abstract, a swastika, the hammer and sickle, a Luger, a Jewish star, and other symbols were set in what appeared to be a whirlwind or tornado, with rocky terrain at its base.

"These are our war memorials. Carved into the base of each are the names of soldiers who did not return to their families. We might be small, but we were not left unscathed."

Cap stepped forward and lowered his head, his mind awash in memories of battles throughout Eastern Europe, including his brief trespass into Carnelia in a fruitless search for Heinrich Zemo.

"I was only here briefly during the war," he said, his voice quiet. "But later, I heard parts of the country got shelled pretty badly. You almost lost Castle Bagsyk . . . I'm glad they missed."

Hordiyenko chuckled. Cap continued, "I gather Stalin always intended to retain Carnelia as part of the USSR. You've really only had a few decades to figure out what you want to be. It's tough to forge your own identity after pledging fealty to others. You know, that's what happened to America. It took years before they could decide on a government that could work for all the people . . . well, most of the people. Then you've been saddled with poor leadership, making you a target. No wonder the prime minister is suspicious."

"She wants strong borders, a strong economy, and mostly she does not want others to tell us what to do," Hordiyenko said.

"No one can blame her," Cap said. "Her distrust of power is understandable. You've seen it misused in the worst possible ways."

"But today, the people also saw what heroism looks like," Hordiyenko said. "They so rarely get to see that."

"I saw the need for all too much of that last time I was here. The weapons being built far outstripped our wisdom to use them. Some cared little for the consequences, seeking power without understanding what that truly meant."

Captain America fell silent, studying the monuments, unaware the exchange had been recorded by some or all of the press. Black Widow had stayed quiet, making herself a human barrier between the two men and the media.

"What can America do to help Carnelia?" Winters asked.

Cap looked up and over at her, suddenly aware of their public surroundings. With a look, Romanova relented and let the press come closer.

"Congresswoman Ojeda is doing that right now, hoping to make Carnelia a trading partner, learning what this country needs and how we might help."

"We're already the world's policeman, what more do we need to do?" Singer challenged.

"Less so, these days," he began slowly. "We have to look after one another—Carnelians, Symkarians, Americans, everyone. We're more fortunate, which gives us the luxury of extending a helping hand when needed."

"All along, someone has been gunning for these countries," Simmons chimed in.

"It's a good thing this is your last stop, then," Captain

Hordiyenko said. "Come, let me show you the memorial topiary." He briskly walked beyond the memorials and the press surged ahead, letting Captain America have a private moment.

"Fear is the only goal being achieved," Black Widow said. "Stir things up in smaller countries."

"You looking for the big bad wolf? Someone trying to gobble them up?"

"Steve, someone is hiring them and turning them loose. The timing is suspect, there must be signals going somewhere, to someone, but right now, it's all guesswork."

"We have Russian mercenaries of a sort with three of the four attackers. Warrior Woman and Gotteskrieger are outliers but likely were hired regardless. Does Russia want their former territories back?"

"If so, why not use the Winter Guard? Why these lesser agents?"

"None of these countries have their own defenses except Symkaria, but Silver Sable and her Wild Pack are a global concern, generating much of the country's revenue. The economies are small; all have been beaten up at one time or another. None are strategic. . . ."

"Except as a buffer to Latveria."

"I don't see the hand of Doom in this, Natasha."

"Thanks to the geography his shadow is so dark, he's the first thought I have each time— and it's not him. We're missing something."

"We're missing a lot of somethings," Cap corrected her. "Who could manipulate S.H.I.E.L.D., allowing the women to break free?"

Natasha Romanova shook her head.

"We need to figure this out before the delegation goes home and forgets what happened here. There's no threat to America, and once they leave Europe, it'll be an unpleasant memory. These people, though, remain vulnerable."

"We're not leaving with them?"

"Not until we figure this out."

As if in response to his query, their comms chirped and they heard the somber voice of Sharon Carter.

"Steve, we're still tracing things, but it appears the request for transfer came from Washington. As best we can determine, the orders came from Europe. Someone from your delegation pulled strings to make it happen.

"You have a traitor in your midst."

CHAPTER EIGHT

Despite Captain America and Black Widow stopping Red Flag from destroying Parliament and a commitment from America to help rebuild the airport, Prime Minister Kamilova was not any happier the following day.

Steve Rogers, though, felt substantially better. He had managed to obtain everything he had needed—a meal, a hot shower, and an excellent deep-tissue massage. Romanova had checked and re-dressed his wounds and he felt more limber. The cracked fingers were still an issue but he'd endure it until the mission was over. Most importantly, he had slept, having received permission to skip the evening reception and climb under the covers early. Almost as good, a S.H.I.E.L.D. courier had flown overnight from Avengers Mansion with a fresh uniform, taking the battered one back to be refurbished.

Physically, he may have been on the mend, but mentally, he was still contemplating Sharon Carter's news from the night before. *A traitor. In their midst.* One of the four delegates was somehow tied to the attacks and was influential in breaking Scattershot and Warrior Woman out.

At breakfast, Rogers sat with Lewin, Gallo, and Jackson while the others—including Romaonva, who was also focused on finding the enemy among them—spoke with cabinet ministers. He reviewed the habits and comments of the four members of Congress, easily dismissing their junior assistants. Ojeda was dedicated and straightforward, while he had grown fond of Jackson. Seaver and Martinez had both kept their distance for reasons he didn't know. He'd been deceived before and it never sat well with him, but he couldn't believe one of them was a turncoat.

"I miss anything last night?" Rogers asked the table as a plate of eggs and sausage was placed before him along with some grilled vegetables. He'd already downed two large glasses of orange juice and was sipping his first cup of coffee.

"Gabby received her first marriage proposal," Gallo said with a chuckle.

"It was rather embarrassing," she said without meeting Rogers' eyes.

"It was hysterical, dude," Gallo said. "Their minister of defense kept hitting on her all night. The more he drank, the better she looked to him until he got down and loudly proposed. It was epic."

"It was humiliating," she said.

"You kept telling her to accept or it'd be a diplomatic incident," Jackson chided Gallo. "You made it worse."

"I was all for diplomatic relations," Gallo chortled.

"More like diplomatic affairs, he's married."

"There! You had a convenient out," Jackson said. "Trust me, I've seen his kind before. You have no idea how many rookies get taken in by a baseball Annie and the next thing you know, their paychecks vanish."

"Sounds like the voice of experience," Gallo said.

"Not me," Jackson said, crossing his heart.

The banter lifted all their moods, not to mention the fact that they were on the penultimate day of the trip. The one expected attack had come, not with a bang, but a rusted whimper. The day would be meetings and tours and would conclude with a state dinner. Years of experience, though, taught Cap not to get too comfortable. Just because they anticipated the previous attack, that didn't preclude a final assault. Much as he would wish it were otherwise, he was always on some level of alert for danger. Black Widow had agreed to stay since Sharon's information the night before meant he would benefit from some help.

It really came down to a matter of timing before they could take the new intelligence and apply it without press attention or causing more European feathers to be ruffled.

"Kamilova was barely in government when all the bad stuff started, so I don't know why she's got a bug up her butt about things," Gallo was saying. Clearly, Cap's mind had wandered and he'd missed part of the conversation.

"She is in charge of a country that has been alternately manipulated and exposed," Jackson said. "Carnelia was under Russia's thumb for so long and since breaking away, they haven't had it easy. This is her first chance to open up and do something positive for her people, but it's undermined by Red Flag and the other attacks. She clearly wants to be independent but is wrapped up in this string."

Just then, Kamilova and Ojeda entered the dining room and were clearly deep in discussion already. Before reaching the occupied tables, the Carnelian stopped and jabbed a finger at the American congresswoman.

"Remember, those Thunderbolts masqueraded as heroes before being exposed as villains. Justin Hammer controlled Iron Man's armor to make it appear he was out of control. What is to say that these so-called attacks are not an illusion, something orchestrated to make us dependent on America or the EU?"

The word "dependent" tugged at Cap's mind.

"I strenuously object," Ojeda said. "We've given you no reason to suspect our intentions."

"No? What about Symkaria? Or Slorenia? Did you leave with good deals that will benefit the American people?" Kamilova said.

"I'd like to think we've gotten started."

"Scare them with an attack and have them come running to you for protection?"

"That's the State Department. We were looking into trade matters, like we are here."

"Trade deals that will come with strings attached, tying us to you, eh?"

And so the two of them went at it again and again, in full view of their comrades but thankfully away from the press. Seaver, though, rose and joined the two, attempting to make peace between them.

"This is breakfast not fight club, come, get some coffee and fruit," Seaver said, placing his hand on the small of Ojeda's back to guide her.

"Madame Prime Minister," Seaver continued, directing his attention to her, "have you tried the *blinchiki*? They added raisins, which I think makes all the difference."

Kamilova stared at the congressman blankly, her irritation slow to seep away.

"Come join me with a plate, you won't regret it," he assured her. The prime minister looked like she wanted to argue but he flashed her a smile that seemed to tip the scales, and she nodded and began walking.

"We have some of the finest kefir in all of Europe, you know," she said with pride. "*That*'s what makes them so good, not the raisins."

"Score one for diplomacy," Jackson said to Rogers.

As he nodded in agreement, Romanova caught his attention and tapped her ear. Clearly, she had received some information that required attention but was not something to be discussed in public. She leaned her head toward the door and he gave her a nod.

She rose and scanned the room. Rogers noticed Seaver leaning in close to the prime minister. It was too close, too intimate, and in an instant he was out of his chair.

"Prime Minister," he called, uncertain what he would say next, hoping Black Widow would pick up the lead.

Kamilova paused and looked directly at Rogers, but he was looking at Seaver, who had yet to move out of her personal space. Something was wrong, very wrong.

"Yes?" she said.

"Seaver, back away," Romanova called, now on her feet.

"What's wrong?" Kamilova asked, trying to back away from Seaver, but he had a solid grip on her arm.

"You're being manhandled by Dmitri Smerdyakov," Black Widow began in response.

"Who?" Kamilova asked.

At the name, Captain America was instantly on the alert. He took a step away from the table, giving him room to move, wishing he had his shield and uniform on. At least, he noted, Romanova was wearing her Widow's Bite bracelets.

"You might recognize him better as the Chameleon."

No one dared move. No one other than Smerdyakov,

who produced an electronic device Cap did not recognize. He presumed it was deadly since its tip was pressed against Kamilova's throat. For her part, the prime minister stood still, eyes wide. She was breathing heavily and Cap hoped she would not panic.

"What's going on?" demanded Ojeda.

"The Chameleon's plan is falling apart and he's getting desperate," Black Widow said. Cap wished he had more intelligence. He trusted she had verified intel and would back her, doing whatever was necessary to save Kamilova's life.

Still using Seaver's voice, Smerdyakov said, "I want safe passage out of this country. You can have her when I'm clear."

"That's not going to happen," Cap said. "Let her go and we'll make a deal with you. You're outnumbered and certainly outgunned beyond those doors."

The Chameleon placed his thumb over a sensor and the device in his hand lit up, casting a ghastly green shadow on Kamilova's face, a low thrum filling the air. Kamilova let out a small squeak.

"I kill her and Seaver gets the blame and you, the great Captain America, look inept. I come out on top either way."

At that moment, the doors burst open and half a dozen Carnelian soldiers filled the space, rifles in position. A corresponding number of scarlet laser dots danced around the Chameleon's chest.

"Stand down," Cap ordered.

"We answer to the prime minister, not America," one man shouted.

"You'll kill her if you open fire," Cap said. "Stand down and let us deal with him."

Kamilova for her part, regained her steel, sneered at her captor, then looked at her soldiers, a small smile of pride crossing her face. She nodded rather than risk speaking and the men lowered their weapons but did not move.

"I'll kill her," the Chameleon repeated in a steady tone, now using his natural voice, the native Russian accent coming through, replacing the Midwestern twang associated with Seaver.

"I believe you," Captain America told him. "But she doesn't need to die. Tell you what, let her go and I will take her place."

"Noble, but you're a trained fighter. I'm no match for you, even with this." The Chameleon gestured with the device, which continued to thrum.

"Okay, Smerdyakov, if we won't grant you safe passage and you won't release the PM, let's try something different. Name your terms."

All the while, Cap stared directly at the Russian impostor, keeping eye contact. He knew full well that by engaging Smerdyakov, Romanova was free to move—slowly—and be ready to act. All he had to do was keep him talking.

"It makes sense, you working with the other congress-men, maintaining the schedule, always the mother hen about being on time. You needed us all there to be witnesses to the attacks even if we were not the targets. We'd confirm the reports, lend American authority to whatever story was going to be spun. You just didn't expect us to take out the agents one by one, did you? Somehow your master thought they would prevail."

Instantly, he realized how true the words were. This *wasn't* Smerdyakov's scheme at all; he was just an opera-tive like they were. So, whoever was behind it still remained unknown. That grated at him.

"You want money? Tech? Gold?" Kamilova asked, con-tempt dripping with every word. "We've suffered worse. We've been overrun. Our ambassador killed on American soil. We've had disgraced prime ministers. We're all replace-able—so kill me and someone else will run the country. You don't scare me."

That seemed to surprise Smerdyakov, who lowered the weapon a few inches away from Kamilova's neck.

Black Widow saw her opportunity and fired her Widow's blast—it struck Smerdyakov's left shoulder. Reflexively, his arm dropped but as it fell, he fired the weapon. A sickly ver-million flash was followed by the squishy sound of impact on flesh.

Captain America spun around and saw Jackson sag, one

hand balancing on the back of a chair, his blue shirt blossoming with red blood. Black Widow crossed the distance to reach Smerdyakov, expertly disarming him, and then knocking him unconscious.

As the soldiers rushed in to form a human shield around Kamilova, Lewin begged the minister she was breakfasting with to summon medical help. Jackson slumped over the chair and Cap caught him with one muscular arm. With great ease, he laid the older man on the floor and used a series of cloth napkins to try to hold back the bleeding, but he'd had years of experience and knew a mortal wound when he saw one. The device would have to be examined but it was clearly some form of . . . death ray, just like Zemo's, not far from the building, in that cavern so long ago.

"Medical help is coming," he reassured Jackson, just to comfort the man.

"I'm not pitching again," Jackson said with a weak smile.

"Afraid not."

"It's bad. It hurts like the dickens and you're not stopping that blood. It's bad."

"It is."

"You have to tell Maggie it was for a good cause. We came to do good."

"Of course."

"Wanted to show you off to the grandkids . . . would've been fun."

They gripped hands, but Jackson's hold was weakening. Behind them, he heard Gallo keeping the area clear and Lewin bellowing for the doctor to hurry. Just then, an older man with a first-aid kit arrived, stethoscope already around his neck. More rushing feet indicated additional medical support coming.

Instinctively, Cap tried to rise and back away, but Jackson held tight, frail as he was. The doctor listened for a brief moment, then tore open Jackson's shirt and began to apply white, gauzy material. As the doctor worked, Cap heard Jackson's breathing grow shallow and intermittent.

He sensed without looking up that Ojeda and Martinez were there, but he also heard Kamilova giving orders, taking charge of the situation. A part of him admired her ability to handle the crisis. Gallo was shooing the press, who had finally responded to the commotion, away from the dining room. There was no word from Black Widow, but he suspected she was remaining with Smerdyakov just in case.

"Steve . . ."

"I'm here."

There was no response and he saw the congressman's chest deflate and the light go out of Al Jackson's eyes.

Captain America was tired. There was no other way to describe the feeling as he and Bucky flew across the English Channel. A US Army captain was accompanying them with the briefing papers and the earnest, younger man seemed in awe of being beside the two costumed fighters. Cap didn't resent the man's admiration, but he also didn't feel like he had earned it. Everyone was fighting and had been for years.

For Steve Rogers, that meant crisscrossing Europe and occasionally being shipped off to the Pacific to deal with one threat after another. In time, Axis soldiers were replaced with an increasing array of mad scientists and their creations. He was created as a counterargument to the Red Skull, who seemed indestructible, but then came Zemo and Strucker and Zola and Nacht and the likes of Baron Blood, Master Man, Warrior Woman, U-Man, Scarlet Scarab, and even the Teutonic Knight.

Rogers' body had taken everything they dished out and he was ready for more. But he was also ready for it to all be over, and it was finally beginning to feel that way. The Soviet army was handing Hitler defeat after defeat, most recently with the Vienna Offensive and the Battle of Königsberg. The *Luftwaffe* was a shadow of its former self and Italy was already under Allied control. The RAF had successfully sunk two more German warships.

Even news from the Pacific was sounding better with the Battle of Okinawa weakening the Japanese forces.

Success was leavened with tragedy, sapping his enthusiasm. First came the realities of the concentration camps as Americans took over Buchenwald, revealing to the world the devastating sight of imprisoned men, women, and children who were little more than skeletons.

Then came the news, just a week earlier, that FDR had died. The last time Cap and Bucky saw the man, he looked unwell, so Rogers was saddened more than surprised. Still, it meant the president was denied the victory he sought for so long. Steve Rogers mourned the man, then daydreamed of peace, and then of finding Peggy Carter in France and renewing their romance.

Turbulence shocked Rogers back to the reality of his situation. The army captain had to repeat the instructions, reviewing the specs on the experimental drone airplane that had been built in secret on a small island in the Channel. German spies, though, had learned of its existence and with their own air forces depleted, couldn't allow automated aircraft to succeed, forever denying the Germans the skies. The Red Skull took the initiative and sent Baron Heinrich Zemo to the island to personally sabotage the drone.

Cap and Bucky were the Allied chess pieces moved on the board to counter the attack.

"Can you picture that, Cap, planes that fly themselves," Bucky was saying with his usual enthusiasm mixed with a dose of cynicism.

"If it means the pilots aren't endangered, it sounds good to me," he responded.

"Think about it, automated planes, then automated warships, and automated tanks. We'd never have to send men to war again. Without men fighting, it really takes the danger out of war."

Cap had to admire Bucky's farsightedness. War would be automated and dehumanized, and it would be easier to launch attacks on one another without stopping to think about the collateral damage. Countless ancient buildings were already gone forever, along with their inhabitants. No, better to fight man to man to never forget the human toll war takes. And takes.

"We can drop you in about five minutes," the captain said, his eyes never leaving his oversized watch.

The soldiers donned their parachutes, checking one another's fitting. They'd done this so often it had become routine, mechanical. Neither would dream of leaving the plane without being certain of the landing.

The captain, whose name Rogers couldn't recall, threw

open the door, the cold wind whipping through the cabin. He resumed looking at his watch but Cap was already surveying the ground. There was a single airstrip and several small buildings plus the hangar. They had few spots to successfully put down without being spotted, so he quickly surveyed them, found one and silently pointed it out to Bucky. There was a confirming thumbs-up and then before the army officer could count down, the two pushed themselves out of the plane.

The free fall before engaging the chute thrilled Cap, even after flying in the arms of the Human Torch and the Sub-Mariner. It was just him, the whoosh of the air, and his companion, and it quickened his heart.

He pulled the rip cord and was yanked up before slowly settling into a drift, which he then expertly controlled so in minutes he safely landed on the grassy spot chosen earlier. He quickly disentangled himself from the chute and placed his shield on his left arm as Bucky made a spot-on landing of his own. Once out of his own harness, he had his rifle in hand.

With practiced silence, the two studied the perimeter, assessing that the British soldiers guarding the drone plane were either dead or imprisoned. The engineers behind the fantastic invention were nowhere to be seen—either dead or also in Zemo's thrall. As they neared the hangar, they both heard unusual mechanical sounds, causing them to pause.

They crept around toward the open hangar entrance and spotted a seven- or eight-foot-tall mechanical man placing something inside a plane. Zemo, wearing a green, fur-lined jacket, watched with delight. Not long before, Cap had thwarted another of his schemes, this involving some super-solution called Adhesive X. In the process, the glue spilled on Zemo's face, permanently affixing a red face mask, which he now adorned with a golden crown. He made a grotesque sight, but really, Cap and Bucky had seen far worse over the last four years.

With his fingers, Cap counted down from five and as the final finger formed a fist, they sprang forward, charging the robot.

What neither had counted on was the amazing speed the machine possessed as it responded quickly to the attack. Incredibly strong arms swung at the pair and swatted them aside like annoying wasps, smashing them both into the side of the hangar and stunning them until Zemo exposed them to a gas that put them to sleep.

The next thing Cap knew, he and Bucky were in army uniforms, strapped to the drone itself. He felt fine now that the noxious gas had dissipated, and he felt the comfort of his shield on his back. The robot was completing securing them to the plane as Zemo watched, adjusting things on a console.

"Be certain that they are bound securely! The führer will

want to behold their lifeless bodies when the captured plane lands in the very heart of Berlin itself!"

"Zemo!"

"Ah, you're awake *Herr Captain*. This is a most fascinating experiment, and if it works, we can rebuild our air force with the designs. We'll have to send Churchill a thank-you note. After all, that's the polite thing to do."

"This plane will never to get Germany," Cap declared.

"Maybe. Maybe not. That's one reason why I added something of my own design to the plane, to ensure it never gets back in the Allies' hands. Either way, you're finished, and that will please both the führer and the Skull. And I will drink a toast to your memory."

With several buttons pressed, the airplane sprang to life as the robot retreated to Zemo's side. The two left the building to get away just in case something went awry. That was the last Captain America would see of the man for decades.

Alone now, Cap realized the plane and his partner were rolling out of the hangar, following its programming, angling toward the runway. They had a minute, two at best, before they were airborne.

The straps the robot had used to secure them to the fuselage were nothing fancy, nor were they as tight as Zemo might have wanted. With his superior strength, Cap was able to stretch the worn fabric, flexing his muscles again and again to either burst or loosen them. In the end, as the plane reached the tarmac, both happened. One strap snapped and another loosened enough for his arms to be free. Quickly he reached around to yank the restraints from his partner. Together, they slid off the plane as it began to gather speed.

"We can't let Hitler get his hands on this," he said.

Bucky pointed to a motorcycle at the side of the hangar. The two men sprinted toward it, jumped on, kicked it into gear, and in seconds were racing after the plane as it made its way toward takeoff. A part of his mind admired that the British science experiment worked and was entirely under its own power. He gunned the engine and the cycle hurried after the speeding plane.

"We're too late, Bucky! We'll have to go after it in another plane!" Cap called, uncertain if there was anything else on the small base.

"No! Don't stop! I think I can reach it, Cap!"

He had to admire the teen's confidence, and his keen mind calculated that if they both leapt in the next few seconds, they could grab onto the tail section just as it began to rise from the ground. The timing would have to be precise—their leap perfect.

Then again, after four years, they had done this sort of thing before, so they both had confidence in success.

"Now!" Cap yelled over the two engines' roar.

The two khaki-clad figures were airborne for several seconds before first one then the other gained a hold on the tail section. The plane continued to rumble forward, flaps working, and suddenly the ground dropped from beneath them. There was the familiar sensation of weightlessness, then Cap's muscles pulled him farther to the middle. Once he had a secure hold on a section, he reached around to give Bucky help. The teen scrambled beside him and found his own piece to hold.

"This is pretty high," he exclaimed.

"We'll be going higher before leveling out. We need to disarm Zemo's device and try to regain control of the drone or ditch it," Cap yelled over the roaring wind.

They shimmied forward, eyes scanning for the added technology and finally, Bucky signaled he spotted it.

"It's got glowing lights and wires, Cap! I have no idea what it's connected to."

"Could be a guidance system of some sort. Can you reach it?"

"I can try." Bucky wriggled ahead of Cap and reached for the device. The plane, though, bucked, and Cap suspected their added weight may have been more than it was designed to carry. They'd be lost over the English Channel if that happened.

"Almost . . ." Bucky said, more to himself than to his partner.

"Be careful, Bucky," Cap warned.

"Almost . . ."

Something changed. A high-pitched beeping began, setting the hairs on the back of Cap's neck at full attention.

"I think it's going to blow," Cap shouted.

"I've got the device!"

"It's too dangerous! Let go and get away from it," the soldier called.

Whether Bucky heard him or not, he was never certain about. He did know that the plane twisted and he let go. He thought—he hoped—Bucky had also let go, with both chancing the icy waters beneath them rather than risk dying with an exploding drone.

A bright light filled his vision as he fell, a wave of heat passed over his uniform front, and a loud explosion rocked his ears. A moment later he felt a splash, some cold, and then everything went black.

CHAPTER NINE

Captain America and Black Widow were conferring with Congresswoman Ojeda about an hour later when they were alerted to a commotion outside Parliament. A young female soldier leaned in and said they had a visitor. Ojeda gestured for the door to be opened.

Silver Sable strode into the conference room, attired in her usual white and silver uniform. She carried a sack cradled under one arm and gave everyone a curt nod of greeting.

"Sable, what brings you here?" Cap asked.

"You think just because you left a mess in my country I was going to sit around and sweep up after you? I've been using my network to do some digging. I've come to share intelligence."

Carefully, she reached into the satchel and withdrew a plain white bag with grease spots adding a polka-dot pattern.

"Sorry they're not still warm, that's when they're best; but they're fresh this morning," she assured Cap.

"Are these . . . ?"

"The word you want is galips. Go ahead and try one."

He reached in and withdrew a sort of circular blob of dough dusted with confectioner's sugar and punctuated with a dot of dark-red jelly at one end. While he wasn't all that hungry, it seemed the polite thing to do, so he took a bite. After one mouthful, he gave his first genuine smile in a while, and wished more than anything for a hot cup of coffee and a ball game to watch.

"Excellent, thanks," he said, finishing the thing in two more bites.

He offered the bag to Black Widow and the congresswoman, who both gingerly took a galip. As they ate, Sable explained her arrival.

"You've certainly been busy," she said. "I've followed each encounter and even I've never heard of Red Flag. They must be running out of names at Super Villain Branding Inc. Anyway, these are all low-level threats. Powerful, yes, but usually not a problem when they rear their ugly faces. I mean, if Darkhawk can take out Psi-Wolf, how difficult a menace can he be?

"We have a bunch of powerful people whose services can be obtained without going broke, so maybe we're dealing with someone with limited means. It could be the real money went to the Chameleon, who's been around a while and would command big bucks. He may be the final piece.

After all, someone has hired these people for a reason. There's been no message, no group claiming credit for the death and destruction they've caused."

"I'm with you so far," Cap assured her, eyeing the bag and considering a second galip.

"There still has to be someone financing the scheme and someone to plan it all out. Chameleon's good but is a bullet, in need of aiming. Maybe the same person, maybe not. That got me to thinking about commonalities."

"Prime Minister Kamilova and President Petrov are both convinced the Russians are behind it," Cap replied. "They've been itching to reassemble some version of the Soviet Socialist Republic."

"Could be, but the Russians are an awfully convenient target," Silver Sable observed. "I have another thought."

* * *

Ojeda had asked Gallo to assemble the press since they were clamoring to learn why Silver Sable had come to Carnelia. A different conference room was set up for the informal press conference, which would be attended by Ojeda, Captain America, and Silver Sable. The local and American media blended together, and there was a burble of multilingual noise as they questioned one another about the eventful week.

Finally, Captain America, in his new uniform, took to the cluster of microphones and appeared ready to speak. At first, the questions were local ones, regarding damage to the streets, personal injuries, and the like. Finally, Winters asked for more details about Congressman Jackson.

"I missed the man's playing career, which I regret. But I got to know him on this trip, and came to respect him for his wisdom and insight. His death is a tragedy because it was an avoidable one, and I take some of the blame for that."

"How could you not realize Seaver was an imposter?" attacked Singer.

"The Chameleon operates successfully *because* of his uncanny ability to assume another identity. I've seen this time and again but there's no 'tell' to look for, nor did we have any reason to think we were infiltrated for what should have been a routine trade trip." Earlier, he had racked his brain to try and figure out how he could have missed this impostor. Then, he slowly came to realize he had spent so much time with Jackson and Ojeda, he hadn't paid as much attention to Martinez and Seaver. As a result, the faux-Seaver was able to operate in the background, keeping them on task without being overt about it. Cap berated himself for not having paid more attention to those around him instead of focusing on external threats.

"Are you suggesting, then, that this Chameleon is behind the attacks?" Simmons asked.

"I don't think he's the architect of these events."

"Then who is?" Singer interjected, echoed by others.

"Why is Silver Sable here? Is Carnelia going to be attacked again?" Simmons asked.

"I have come to stand beside my American colleague," Sable put in before Cap could reply. "While he's been protecting multiple countries, I have been investigating."

"What have you learned?" Winters asked.

"There's been one person plotting all of these attacks, and he has done so in the employ of another party . . ."

Sable was interrupted by shouts from reporters throwing out the names of countries from Latveria to Sin-Cong. As Sable waited them out, the noise subsided until finally, one voice remained.

"Or don't you know at all and you're bluffing?" Singer needled.

Silver Sable gave Melissa Singer a cold, deadly smile. "I don't bluff, Ana."

There was a momentary pause as the other press thought Silver Sable merely misspoke the journalist's name. Cap heard the name and began reviewing opponents with that name, not sure who Silver Sable indicated. But then Singer curled her lip and dropped the recorder she had been using. As it struck the carpet, it flared with a brilliant, white light along with an ear-splitting crack.

At the sound of the camouflaged flash-bang, Captain

America darted to his left, Silver Sable to her right as they tried to flank the woman. They had expected something of this nature and were not fazed as they moved through the bewildered crowd with ease. The woman called Ana, though, did not flee and positioned herself, ready to fight. With the reporters still in the room, Cap had to rethink his fighting tactics and slung his shield behind him, flexing his still sore but mostly functional muscles.

Ana jabbed her right hand at his neck, fingers extended, landing several rapid-fire blows in succession. She was clearly an expert at Krav Maga and was going to demonstrate her mastery in an attempt to quickly take down the Star-Spangled Avenger. With lightning-fast speed, she switched to grab his right wrist and tried to use his momentum against him while he, instead, used his great weight against her. Ana backed off with a Russian curse on her lips.

That convinced Captain America that he was really fighting Ana Kravinoff, daughter of the deadly Russian hunter Kraven. It was all starting to fall into place.

Whirling, she let out a vicious kick that caught the sailing Silver Sable in the shoulder, sending her backward into the screaming press. Turning her attention back to Captain America, Kravinoff snatched a camera tripod and brandished it as a weapon, spinning it before her, its collapsible legs trying to entangle Cap's arms.

The Avenger ducked under the weapon, slid between her splayed legs, braced himself with his hands and swiveled his legs up, catching her in the face. Kravinoff reeled with the blow, but used the opportunity to get some distance from Cap. Instead, though, she was now within Sable's reach. The two women exchanged some rapid-fire punches and kicks, a brutal dance that Cap dared not cut in.

He took the opportunity to herd the journalists out of the room, letting them pass beyond the cordon of armed soldiers, ensuring the battle would be contained. Of course, they wanted to stay and record the confrontation, so he wound up being a little harsher with them than he intended. Thankfully, Gallo and Lewin were out in the corridor, and worked to move the press corps away.

Meanwhile, Kravinoff performed a leg sweep that tangled up Sable, who went down hard. The attacker was ready to bounce on top of her when a red-gloved hand grabbed her instead and threw her heavily into a wall. Stunned, she fell to the carpet and tugged at her earring. With a flick, she sent it toward the windows, which shattered as the earring exploded. As Cap reacted, and Silver Sable got to her feet, Ana leapt to her feet and hurled herself through the aperture.

The Russian hit the street outside of Parliament and got her bearings for a second before turning to run. Soldiers were positioned on the street but had scattered at the explosion and remained in disarray. She could take advantage of that.

A black hand punched out and connected with her jaw, sending her spinning. Righting herself, she saw Black Widow crack her knuckles in anticipation. Behind her, Cap landed on the shattered glass, crunching it beneath his boots. Then a second set of footsteps: Silver Sable.

The three surrounded Ana, but the woman was clearly not about to surrender. They did, though, wait her out. They moved as she moved, tense and ready to pounce if another weapon was deployed.

From around them came more sounds—heavy trucks, boots, the snap of cameras, the hubbub of a crowd, shouts from the police and security forces to stay back. Cap concentrated on the sounds, making certain all was secure before they reengaged.

Ana leapt high, her feet wrapping around Sable's neck, her arms reaching for Black Widow, and she yanked them both off their feet as she spun and landed. Cap charged her as she did so and delivered an uppercut that missed. Her reflexes, he knew, were sharp. Something seemed wrong, though; her body seemed to be rippling, which was not what he was expecting. Suddenly, green tendrils burst through her shirtsleeves and pant legs, writhing in the air. Several slid out of her collar and wrapped around her face.

Well, this is new, he considered. The tendrils resembled

vines and seemed to stretch about a yard out. Rapidly, he recalculated how he intended to fight her as he placed his shield on his arm—in case they exuded poison or something worse.

"Stay back," he commanded, heading for Ana.

"You won't be able to stop me on your own," she said, now displaying a Russian accent.

"That's okay, my backup will be sufficient," he told her.

She lunged forward, several of the tendrils leading, and while he blocked several with his arms, the ones from her legs wrapped around him and pulled him close. Then his arms were pinned against him and she gave a command and the tendrils squeezed with plenty of pressure, enough so he felt it through his chain mail.

Silver Sable tossed several of her crescent-shaped *chais* at the tendrils while withdrawing her ever-present sword.

One *chai* bit into a tendril, causing Ana to scream in pain. It also meant the tendrils reflexively released Cap and writhed in the air, reacting to the stimuli. Ana triggered something on her bracelet and everyone braced for a detonation, electric charge, or something else. When nothing happened, they studied her while she bit down on the pain and smiled coldly.

"You're not the one with backup," she said.

"The Chameleon," Black Widow said, not even waiting for confirmation. She broke into a dead run for Parliament and the containment space set up for the criminal impostor.

Cap saw Ana remained slow to move from the pain inflicted by the chai, which she removed. To throw her off guard, he threw himself into a forward roll, getting close to her, and then sprang up with another powerful uppercut, this one catching her on the point of her chin and sending her backward to the concrete.

Once she hit the ground, Sable was standing with her sword out, threatening two of the tendrils toward the base, at Ana's thighs.

"Surrender, Ana, it's over."

"Not in the slightest," Ana said.

Cap tapped his helmet, activating comms and as the connection was made, he heard Black Widow say the Chameleon had gassed his guards and escaped. Worse, he'd grabbed one of their tablets and managed to reach out to someone or something. It clicked in his mind that perhaps disabling the S.H.I.E.L.D. Helicarrier was actually a part of their contingency plans.

At that, a low roar was heard in the distance, and he watched as a compact jet plane, the design of which he did not recognize, rose from behind a cluster of buildings.

"You may have me, but we have a plane and it is filled with a deadly toxin. Release me or the pilot will follow his instructions and poison everyone in Carnelia."

"Including yourself," Sable told her.

"Maybe," was all Ana would say.

"I've got her, you go," Sable said.

But he was already moving faster than she imagined.

The Star-Spangled Avenger bolted from the parliament building and spotted an SUV and its driver across the street. He ran toward the vehicle and shouted, hoping the man understood English, "Drive me to that jet!" The man looked up, spotted the plane, then broke into a gap-toothed grin and gave the hero a thumbs-up. Cap was already jumping to grasp the running board, holding on to the passenger-side mirror. The vehicle's engine roared and with a jolt, they moved swiftly down the street.

"Natasha, what do you know about the toxin?" he asked over the comms. The vehicle's tires squealed as they rounded a corner, the jet now dead center but afar.

"I'm willing to bet it's the same one Red Flag was carrying. It may be why she hired him."

"It certainly wasn't for that name," interrupted Sharon Carter. "We're running data on the toxin now."

"I'm not sure we have time for jokes, but I do wish you were here," Cap said. The jet was gaining altitude, well beyond shield range, and beginning to circle the capital city.

"Me too. Our intelligence shows that if airborne the toxin will affect all human life in at least a dozen mile radius, killing adults within twenty-four hours, children and seniors faster."

"Does Yesenofsky have a cure?" The vehicle slowed down, uncertain where to go, when Cap rapped on the roof and the SUV lurched forward, gaining speed once more. The jet grew closer and Cap was already thinking of ways to reach it.

"His father developed the toxin and he's merely a victim," Carter said.

"Does S.H.I.E.L.D. have a sample for analysis? Can you create a cure?"

"We may be S.H.I.E.L.D., but we're not God. We have intelligence on this because we've tracked his father, Sergei Yesenofsky . . ."

"Doctor Yes," Black Widow added.

"Seriously?"

"Focus, Steve."

"His father was once head of biological weapons for the Soviet Union," Black Widow recalled. "He's been a global terrorist creating one toxin after another along with increasingly sophisticated androids. All to finance repairs for his son's armor. He's also been rather unlucky."

"How so?" Cap asked.

"When he tried to unleash Deathbringer 8000 in Times Square he was stopped by Squirrel Girl."

Carter chuckled loudly at that.

"Don't dismiss Doreen," Cap warned. "She's surprisingly effective. It's why she's an Avenger."

"Steve, wait, we have the Deathbringer toxin. If we analyze that, I bet we can come up with a cure that might work on an earlier iteration."

"How long?"

There was a long silence and he knew that it would take far too long to study the deadly concoction then craft and test a possible cure. Given the country's small size, the vast majority of the population would be infected plus, no doubt, neighboring countries would also be stricken. This could be far more destabilizing than a series of random attacks. But, he realized, it was not the main plan. Whoever was behind this scheme did not want a high death toll. The culprit wanted something else.

"Kamilova wants to evacuate the city," Romanova interrupted.

"There'd be mass panic and honestly, it won't do any good. We have to neutralize the jet before it disperses the toxin. Is the Helicarrier near?"

"Not close enough to do us any good," Sharon Carter said.

"Natasha, is Ana secure?"

"Yes." He'd doubt that reassurance had it come from anyone other than Black Widow. "We have her trussed up and used a mild sedative to make sure her appendages remain inactive."

Rogers was interrupted by a loud engine sound from

behind. Fearing an attack, he angled the mirror to look behind him only to see Silver Sable quickly closing the distance between them. She throttled back her jet pack and was pacing the car.

"Silver, will you lend me the jet pack? I have to stop the plane."

"I am perfectly capable of doing that myself," she said, her face showing her displeasure at the notion.

"I'm not saying that. I am saying that the super-solider serum might help me should I be exposed to the toxin. If you caught a whiff, it'd be fatal and Symkaria needs you."

"I'll take the shield as collateral," she said with a wicked smile.

She silently flew ahead a block and landed gracefully. Sable was already unbuckling the harness when Cap jumped from the SUV.

He slipped the shield from his shoulders and handed it to her. Hefting it in her hands for the first time, she admired its curvature and balance. "I have to try and make some of these for my team."

"Others have tried, but this is one of a kind," he said.

"So are you."

Cap quickly donned the jet pack with its oversized blue fuel tanks as Sable adjusted straps and fittings. She showed him the hand controls that nearly did not fit over his larger, red-gloved hands.

"With your mass, I suspect you can do up to three-thousand feet and have about twenty-five minutes of fuel. Your max speed will be two hundred and fifty miles per hour but you can't sustain that for long. This is not a finesse mission, but life and death. Force it down, disable the release ports, whatever it takes, but don't be fancy," she admonished.

Satisfied, she nodded he was ready.

"Thanks, Silver. You better get back to the others. Ana Kravinoff is deadly, even in captivity."

"You don't trust Black Widow to handle her?"

"Of course, but we've been surprised and sucker punched for a week now. I won't rule anything out."

With that, he depressed a palm button and the twin tanks belched a red-yellow flame. Suddenly, he was off the ground and gaining altitude so fast he felt a dropping sensation in his stomach. The feeling, though, immediately brought back memories. It had been a motorcycle and an allied plane, but he couldn't help but reimagine his and Bucky's leap onto the drone as it left the British island.

He had hoped for the element of surprise, but as he neared five hundred feet, the pilot spotted him, banked the jet, and headed to the west at a speed Cap couldn't hope to match. Still, he had to get closer to goose the engines and felt the wind tear at his cheeks as he sped up, closing the distance.

The jet twisted, turned, and was now coming at the

speeding Avenger. Cap had used jet packs before, but this was a brute-force pack, with little in the way of dynamic control. Times like this, he wished he had a spare set of the Falcon's wings. He did understand he needed to make himself a small target, though, so tried to adjust his angle to remain a head-on approach.

Which is when the jet opened up with twin-mounted machine guns. Tracer bullets flared in the sky, two bright orange lines slicing through the blue sky.

Several of the first shots struck him, flattening against the Kevlar-lined chain mail, but they stung and would leave bruises to this growing list of injuries on this "goodwill" trade tour. A lucky shot nicked his right leg and it hurt, but he just gritted his teeth and ignored the pain, just like all the others.

Cap tapped the controls and shot straight up for a few seconds, gaining altitude and avoiding the bullets. The plane zipped by his former position. This allowed him to twist, turn, and enter pursuit.

The jet zigzagged at high speed, preventing the hero from catching up, let alone getting close enough to grab hold. As it flew, he made mental snapshots of the structure, noticing the series of red and yellow rectangular objects affixed to the fuselage and along the wings. That had to be the toxin and the pilot was killing time until Ana Kravinoff sent the signal to disperse the gas into the air over the city.

How long would she have given them?

"Sit rep," he practically screamed into his mic, hoping he could hear the replies.

"Ana's sleeping it off," Romanova said.

"Kamilova is furious at everyone and everything," Sable added. "She wants to launch her air force against it."

"How long do we have?"

"She never said."

"Just swell."

"Where's the jet?"

"Northwest quadrant of the city, firing bullets but not releasing the gas," he told them.

"S.H.I.E.L.D. estimates support to arrive in twenty-two minutes," Sharon Carter added. "Can you stop the plane or at least stall it?"

"He won't have enough fuel," Sable said.

"Then I guess I have to stop it now," he said.

"Steve, how are you going to do that?"

"Same as always, Sharon. Perseverance."

"And luck," Sable said.

"I never count on that," Cap said. "Maybe I make my own, but it's never in the tactical plans."

He went radio silent, focusing on the pilot's tactics, having already noted he always banked left first, always made clockwise circles, and never got too close. With that knowledge and having finally gotten a good feel for the jet pack, he formulated a plan, mentally drawing a grid in the sky, anticipating the pilot's next few moves and making his own corresponding actions.

With a twist of the controls, he regained height, but was at an angle seemingly heading for nowhere in particular. The pilot could clearly see the figure dart upward and sure enough, banked left, nose angled upward, readying to fire once more.

What he didn't count on was Cap forming a parabolic arc that had him now rushing directly at the rear of the jet at the pack's top speed.

The jet tried to move out of the way, but was caught off guard and the Sentinel of Liberty made a rough impact with the tail section, both gloved hands cutting his engine, then grabbing onto the tail with iron muscles and will.

The pilot went into evasive maneuvers designed to shake the man loose from the jet. Instead, Cap's mighty muscles held tight and in fact, managed to inch him forward. Then, the next time the pilot tried to circle, Cap grabbed the tail section, activated his pack and the extra thrust forced the plane into a spin.

As the pilot fought to control the spin and regain altitude, Captain America moved forward. The g-forces were terrific, far worse than the first time he tried to disable a plane in flight during the Second World War, when they flew at slower speeds. Back then, he had to worry about Zemo's explosive, the drone's delicate controls, and Bucky.

Here, it was just him and the pilot. And a plane full of deadly toxin.

The pilot stopped attempting to extricate the Avenger from the plane and tried to head back toward the city. Instead, Cap made one desperate gamble, activating Sable's jet pack once more and letting the engine and his control of the tail section prove the difference. As they cleared the city, a large lake came into view.

His keen mind silently counted down, and then he leapt from the jet, the jet pack still roaring. A warning beep told him he was getting dangerously low on fuel. He looped around the jet once, then on the second pass positioned himself below the rear and, with his arms stiff, rammed into the fuselage. The jet suddenly dipped, its nose directed at the ground. More specifically, at the lake.

The beeping grew faster and louder.

The lake, placid and reflecting the oncoming jet set against a beautiful blue sky, rapidly grew in size.

The jet pack sputtered once then went silent.

The pilot, no doubt a hireling, wasn't ready to die and ejected, possibly too low to safely land, but the risks outweighed trying to survive the watery crash.

The plane shuddered as the canopy flew off and the ejection seat and its occupant were spit high into the air.

With no more thrust to keep him in position, Cap let go of the plane, which was now a missile heading for the lake.

He hoped it was a good, deep one. Its circumference suggested it would be sufficient.

Cap tumbled away from the plane. Unlike when he fell from the drone, he was in control. He didn't have to worry about losing anyone this time. He didn't have to relive watching his partner and best friend perish in the Atlantic Ocean. In the seconds left to him, Cap opened the latches and wriggled out of the now useless jet pack. He twisted a bit to adjust his angle of descent to ensure he was nowhere near the jet. Then, he put his hands together before him and with legs completing the straight line, became a human torpedo.

The jet, its engines still engaged, struck the water first, sending up a huge plume of water and smoke. As the nose hit, the entire plane flipped over before sinking, exposing its belly and the lethal packages.

Cap struck the water seconds later, piercing the surface and going deep. He kept his eyes closed, held his breath, and then leveled out for a moment. He tried to sense if the plane was on fire or if the toxin had been released but everything was oddly quiet. He felt the ripples of the heavy metal object begin to sink, but nothing else.

Arms at his sides, he shimmied his hips, kicking with his powerful legs and headed for the surface.

His head broke through and he took a careful sniff before releasing his breath. He knew he had time to test the air before having to breathe in. The air was acrid from engine fuel but nothing else was noticeable.

Exhaling, he noted the pilot had tumbled into the water and was fighting with his parachute but was otherwise unharmed.

He then took in a deep lungful of air, which was cool and refreshing.

"Cap!"

"Steve!"

Comms still worked so he smiled at the worry in Romanova's and Sharon's voices. "I'm fine. The jet hit the lake and the toxin is intact. We owe Silver for her jet pack, that's gone."

"She says she's keeping the shield."

He chuckled at Black Widow's comment and then asked to be collected, and for police to take custody of the pilot. Then, turning on his back, he floated and let himself rest. The fresh aches and bruises kept him awake, asking for attention, but the first-aid kit was miles away, so they'd just have to wait patiently.

He floated, just breathing.

Unlike that crash in the ocean back in '45, the water was nowhere near as cold.

CHAPTER TEN

Hours later, Prime Minister Kamilova convened an unusual meeting in her private residence. Her drawing room, normally empty except for holidays, was now filled with an assortment of foreigners the likes of which she never imagined. Her security forces insisted on sweeping the house for bugs, explosives, and intrusive cameras (beyond the ones she had installed herself). The press—both local and foreign—were promised a press conference later that evening, one that was no doubt going to be live around the world.

But for now, it was just her and her guests: Captain America, Black Widow, Silver Sable, and the surviving delegates, Ojeda and Martinez. There was an urn of coffee but most in the room opted instead for the liquor selection, filling their tumblers and settling on couches and chairs.

"Can someone please explain for me exactly what just happened to my country? There's no press, no other government, just us. I'd appreciate some honesty."

"I'm afraid we've been as candid as possible all along,

Madam Prime Minister," Ojeda said, her voice demonstrating the strain that had taken its toll on her, notably the death of her colleague.

"She's telling you the truth," Cap said, hoping his reputation earned him Kamilova's attention. "Ever since this junket began, at each stop there has been attack. There has been no real connection between Scattershot, Psi-Wolf, Warrior Woman, Gotteskrieger, and Red Flag . . ."

"Such horrid names," Kamilova interjected.

"That may well be, but other than their appearance being low on the terrorism watch lists, there's been no previous connection. Now we know the Chameleon has been acting as their front man, assuring our presence at each attack, making it appear we were involved or complicit or something."

"Was he responsible for those women attacking your plane?"

Captain America shook his head. "Those orders came from elsewhere." He put his coffee cup down. "We traced the sequence of events, which, thanks to American bureaucracy, took some time to unwind. From the best intelligence we can gather, this has been in the planning stages for some time. It appears the Chameleon replaced Seaver in Washington, a week prior to our departure, giving him time to be fully briefed on the delegation's plans and to acclimate himself to the role."

Ojeda's hand flew to her mouth. "We took three votes that week!" she said. "They're now invalid."

"There were substantial margins in all three," Martinez said quietly. "Discount his votes and the bills still pass. But, how did he manage to free those women?"

"It appears that the Chameleon, as Seaver, contacted people at the Justice Department and arranged for an American request to have Scattershot and Warrior Woman remanded to US custody, for them to stand trial on older warrants before new ones could be filed. When S.H.I.E.L.D. gets a request from the US attorney general, arms get twisted and the wheels put in motion. The executive director was unaware of these machinations. Were they meant to be freed for an escape or for a chance to put them back into play? We're not sure."

Kamilova wrote some notes, shaking her head.

"What about this. . . " Kamilova paused to check a series of hastily written notes, ". . . Anastasia Tatiana Kravinoff?"

"Her father is Sergei Kravinoff, a brilliant hunter and occasional criminal known as Kraven the Hunter. Do you know of him?"

Kamilova shook her head.

"He has been a thorn in Spider-Man's side for some time. For a while, it appeared he had taken his life and Ana blamed Spider-Man for her father's death. She came to America in search of revenge and has been around ever since. And her father was alive, after all. The daughter, unlike Kraven, appears to have super-human speed and strength. Couple that with being trained by her father, she is a world-class martial artist, marksman . . ."

"Markswoman," corrected Ojeda.

"Amateur," Black Widow scoffed.

"She is a brilliant hunter and tracker, a superb strategist," Cap continued. "It's said she is also quite versatile with exotic poisons and the like."

"What of those tentacles?" Ojeda asked.

"S.H.I.E.L.D. is uncertain, but they suspect somewhere on her mother's side of the family there are Inhuman genes, so when the Terrigen cloud found her, she became one of the Nuhumans."

"In fact, she dropped off the grid shortly after the new appendages appeared," Black Widow added.

"Who is behind this and what they want is what has been bothering us all because whatever it is, well, it's not obvious."

"Are you so sure, Captain?"

"Ma'am?"

"This Ana Kravinoff, you say she is a genius tactician, so is she not behind this?"

"No," Black Widow said, finishing her drink. "Ana is young, schooled in her craft by her father, but has never espoused a particular ideology. She also learned at the knee of her uncle, the Chameleon."

"Are you joking? They're family?" Kamilova asked.

"I am not joking, Madame Prime Minister. We didn't

even know of her existence until the world thought Kraven was dead and she came to America to exact revenge against Spider-Man."

"Are they working together?"

"No. Father and daughter appear somewhat estranged at present, as she has not seen him since her transformation. In fact, she helped the Inhumans briefly, then vanished until now."

"You think someone hired her?" Ojeda asked.

"Yes. Ana has funds but nothing like what must have been spent to hire these mercenaries, in addition to manufacturing the toxin, outfitting the jet, and hiring that pilot S.H.I.E.L.D. fished from the wreckage in your lake, and based on their analysis we're able to track it. The jet surreptitiously followed each attack. Ana always had it on hand as a fail-safe should something go wrong."

"But why impersonate a journalist?" Ojeda asked.

"By coming along, she could observe and adjust. Also, she was filing reports back home that were hostile to our mission, sowing some discontent to further undermine American influence."

"Our vetting practices for the press have to be tightened," Ojeda murmured to herself.

"Why Carnelia?" Kamilova asked no one in particular.

"Why Symkaria, Transia, and Slorenia?" Silver Sable asked.

"You are all formerly connected to the USSR but are not landlocked together," Ojeda said. Heads nodded at that.

"My people should suffer for the past?"

"Many cultures hold grudges, seeking retribution from innocents," Captain America said softly.

"Where do we go from here, Prime Minister?" Ojeda asked. "There are two funerals I need to prepare for."

"Carnelia owes America some thank yous, I believe," Kamilova said. "After that, we will reschedule the trade talk."

"You should come with me to Slorenia," Ojeda said. "We can show some unity."

"Unity," Silver Sable said and looked at Black Widow. The two women seemed to be communicating something to one another, something Cap could guess at, but not with certainty.

"When will S.H.I.E.L.D. remove Kravinoff from Carnelia?"

"I've been assured she can be collected whenever you want," Black Widow said.

"She won't stand trial here?" Ojeda asked.

"We are small and ill equipped for a super-villain circus. Yes, she and the Chameleon committed crime and murder here, and threatened my people, but we will ask the International Criminal Court to deal with this mess since their crimes cover multiple countries."

Silver Sable and Black Widow once more exchanged looks but Cap was too tired and too sore to get their message.

"Your country was once a USSR satellite," Silver Sable said.

"As was Symkaria, no?"

"No, Prime Minister. Almost, but we were lucky to avoid being absorbed. Slorenia, though, was under Russia's thumb since the eighteenth century, and Transia was nearly taken over, but the superstitious avoided it rather than tempt Chthon."

"Chthon?" Kamilova asked.

"A demon trapped within Wundagore Mountain," Silver Sable said as if describing the weather. How bizarre their world was, Cap thought, not for the first time.

"That's not a legend?"

"Sorry, no. All have been independent for a while now, but events elsewhere have shown time and again that the smaller countries suffer the greatest without heroes of their own. Russia has plenty of heroes and land, so I don't think they're behind this."

"Then who?" Kamilova demanded.

"We live in a world of super beings—gods, mutants, Inhumans, Eternals, and aliens. Many work to preserve life, others to exploit or destroy it. All four lands have been impacted one way or another because of their size, lack of Russian protection, and desirable resources. Who would benefit from them all forming a federation?"

"A noncontiguous one?" Ojeda asked.

"Unite these four and you can just about go from the Baltic to the Aegean. You box out Latveria and suddenly have some heft to negotiate with both the EU and Russia."

"And you think these attacks were to do what exactly?" Kamilova scribbled furiously on her pad, trying to keep up, even going so far as to quickly sketch Europe and place dots roughly where the four countries were located.

"Instill fear. Reinforce the instability of the world order and the need for alliances. Other than the UN, these four countries are not part of NATO or any other alliance. You've valued your independence, but that has come with a price, one each of you have paid time and again. With the four of you signing a pact, others would be tempted to join you. Being small and independent may no longer look so desirable."

"Unless you're Wakanda," Ojeda said.

"I'd love their resources," Kamilova said.

"And Black Panther stands to protect them. But who stands to protect Carnelia when you're overrun by Chitauri or Lemurians?"

"Lemurians?" Ojeda said.

"Later. She's on a roll," Cap whispered to her.

"No one. Slorenia has, at best, a mutant named Locomotive Breath. The Knights of Wundagore protect the mountain, not the country."

"But, if the four countries have a mutual protection pact

of some sort . . ." Kamilova said hesitatingly, trying to work it through.

"Then you have me," Silver Sable said. "The Wild Pack and I would be engaged to protect our new allies."

"For a fee," Black Widow said.

"So, the one who benefits is Symkaria. But this was not the king's doing; he's a good man," Cap began. "No, it has to be someone toward the top . . . someone like . . . Artem Tartaryn, the prime minister."

There were confirming nods around the room as the reality of their conclusion settled over them.

"He was making a big deal out of their size when we were visiting," Martinez noted.

"Trying to deflect attention perhaps," Cap said.

"Why do all this during the American tour?" Kamilova asked.

"To show that not even Captain America can keep everyone safe," Ojeda said. "It wasn't about us at all. It was because we invited you along, Cap."

"Once it was announced he would be part of the tour, the plan was put in place by Tartaryn," Black Widow said. "He would have already hired Kravinoff to put the scheme together, using Symkarian funds to hire the mercenaries. To make certain Captain America was on hand, they needed someone on the inside, so someone, either Kravinoff or Tartaryn, brought in the Chameleon."

"Where is the real Seaver, then?" Ojeda asked, suddenly realization plain on her stricken face.

"S.H.I.E.L.D. is working with the FBI on just that," Cap reassured her. As soon as Smerdyakov was exposed, Rogers contacted Sharon Carter, so the hunt was already underway. It was not like the Chameleon to kill his targets, so there was a great likelihood Seaver would be found alive.

"But Captain America stopped each attack," Kamilova said, still coming up to speed on the dizzying revelations and conclusions.

"Yes, but after the attacks had begun and there was substantial property damage. The Transian president's wife and son was their biggest miscalculation," Cap said.

"Symkaria would annex or ally their neighboring countries and protect their people and lands. They'd hem in Latveria, protecting themselves long term and gain better bargaining power around the world."

When Sable finished speaking, the room fell silent. It made a sickening sense but it also meant Tartaryn would have to be brought to justice. Cap knew it would hurt her to arrest one of her own countrymen, so he excused himself to the hall to confer with Sharon. They'd need to brief the king while obtaining an international warrant for S.H.I.E.L.D. to arrest the prime minister. There was a brief conversation over who would have to notify the king and both decided it had to come from Sable, even if she did not perform the arrest.

Rogers returned to the room to see everyone had refilled their glasses and had already turned their attention to the press conference. Who would speak; who did this horrible news sound better coming from? Ojeda recognized that America was an invited guest and a witness, but the news couldn't come from there. It was a local problem, so it was agreed Kamilova and Silver Sable would make a joint appearance.

The meeting broke up and Kamilova suggested they reconvene an hour prior to the press conference with the other Americans for a farewell meal. That gave Cap time for a quick nap, which his battered body would find most welcome. Once he got home, he swore he'd take a day off and go to the movies. Something simple and normal. Something he so rarely did but had fought across time to preserve the freedom to do.

At the dinner, Ojeda briefly outlined the scheme, the news that Tartaryn had already been arrested, and that just Ojeda would attend the Transian funeral on behalf of the United States. Kamilova confirmed the rulers from the affected countries would also show up as a sign of sympathy and unity. No one missed the irony that Tartaryn's scheme might actually become real, but without the need for bloodshed or destruction.

Once the recap was completed, the mood lightened considerably as the Americans, Black Widow, Silver Sable, and the Carnelian prime minister enjoyed local delicacies and Transian wine.

"You know, we're going to be investigated for this trip," Martinez said. "Too much happened, so some grandstanding committee chair will want to make an example of us."

"An example of what?" Gallo challenged. "We came with good intentions."

"And didn't show the good sense to come home after the first attack," Martinez shot back, eyeing Ojeda. It was clear to Cap that the man blamed her for Jackson's death. In a partisan Congress, no one disliked Jackson.

"The paperwork," Lewin moaned into her third glass of wine.

"The price of government," Cap told her, carefully removing the glass before it spilled.

"Too high if you ask me," Gallo said. "We need a paper-reduction act."

"Pick one," Martinez said.

"Huh?"

"There was one in 1942, another in 1965, then 1980, with an amendment in 1995," Martinez said. "When I proposed one during my freshman year, I got laughed out of committee."

Gallo merely groaned at that.

"How do you feel, Cap?" Lewin asked.

"I've been better, but not too bad, thanks."

"I wish I could have done something," she complained. "All I did was run, or cower, or calm down the press. They're ornery." She betrayed a bit of a drawl, and he couldn't tell if it was an affectation or genuine.

"You did your part and I did mine," he assured her. Not that he felt all that assured by his words. Yes, he had tried his best, but there was still death, near death, and millions in destruction these small, frail countries could ill afford. Even banded together, they would struggle in the increasingly competitive global economy.

After dinner, everyone took their positions out of sight of the press as Silver Sable and Prime Minister Kamilova took their places before the cameras, the Carnelian flag acting as their backdrop. Both were in fresh outfits, picture perfect and professional. The prime minister read a prepared statement she had written herself based on the afternoon's notes. She outlined what had happened in the four countries, who was responsible, and why this happened.

"King Stefan has confirmed that his former prime minister is in custody while Sharon Carter, running the op for S.H.I.E.L.D., says the super-powered mercenaries are under their control until everyone stands trial.

"But first we must all mourn. We mourn the death of President Petrov's wife and son, and for the American congressman, Al Jackson. Our nation will fly its flag at half mast this week and I will attend funerals for both.

"Then we will heal. We will examine what motivated a nationalist to commit such crimes across Europe. We will look at his causes and reasons and see if anything good can come from this," Kamilova concluded extemporaneously.

Questions flew fast and furious, about national sovereignty, about American interference, about reprisals against Symkaria. None of the questions surprised Cap as he heard them. Without Ana in their midst, the tenor was less belligerent, although still vigorously inquisitive. Kamilova responded to most of them, although Cap appreciated Silver Sable's defense of America.

"Earlier today, I was given a priceless object as collateral for the loan of Symkarian technology," Sable said. "The jet pack Captain America used was lost in the battle to protect Carnelia so, technically, his shield is now my property. But, frankly, it doesn't go with my outfit." There were some chuckles at the joke. "No, it was given in friendship and in a similar act, I return the shield to the one man who best knows how to use it to defend."

At a gesture, a Carnelian army officer walked to the podium carrying the shield, freshly polished. Then she beckoned Captain America to come from backstage and he strode forward. She gave him the shield and the cameras blindingly flashed for a long while.

Cap turned to go, then spun about, shield still on his

arm, and looked at the microphones. Kamilova nodded her head and Cap stepped forward.

"I have been here before; I have walked across Europe to protect the idea of freedom, to protect those who cannot defend themselves. During the Second World War, it was very clear who was the enemy. It was anyone who used fear to replace leadership with control. It was anyone who wanted to limit freedom in any form. We took up arms to protect a way of life and the Symkarian way is different from the Transian way, but the Allies protected your right to choose the manner in which you lived.

"Today, it's far more complicated as external forces add pressure. We have, for better or worse, become a central hub for intergalactic, interdimensional, and interspecies activity. We have our own issues to worry about, from famine to clean water, and there are many who seek to impose their will on others. Some continue to use fear of the unknown, the fear of the different to try and manipulate events.

"People can be manipulated in so many different ways that it becomes increasingly difficult to judge what is fact, what is fiction, and who is trying to help or hurt you. As a result, trust has been eroded to the point where it has become one of our most precious and rarest commodities. Trust has to be earned and it's earned not through words but through deeds. The congressional delegation came to improve ties between America and these four countries. There will be trade, which will help all. They are acting. When your countries were attacked, I did what I was trained to do: protect. And when the odds looked tough, I received voluntary aid. I didn't ask for Black Widow to come to Europe, and she didn't let her worldview enter into the equation. She saw a threat and came running. The same with Silver Sable, who normally is hired for such work. But here, she came for the good of all.

"We saw people and property endangered. We acted. Hopefully, our acts show our sincerity, our belief that we do not have the right to impose our will on you. Instead, everyone in Symkaria, Transia, Slorenia, and Carnelia will decide what is best for them and let their leaders guide that will.

"Know this: whatever you decide, whatever choices you make will not stop us from coming to your aid when necessary. It's a big, scary world out there and we do not have ideology checklists to determine who needs protecting or avenging. No strings. No charge. Decide what is best for you and sleep easily, knowing we will continue to stand guard."

With a nod to Kamilova, Rogers turned and walked from the podium, ignoring the questions hurled his way. Instead, he went backstage, avoiding the others, and took a seat in the shadows. For a moment, just for a brief moment, he knew the fight was done for the day. It wasn't over, it would never be over. No doubt, when he tried to go to the movies the following day, some new menace would keep him from his popcorn. But right now, the battle was over and he was going to savor the moment.

ACKNOWLEDGMENTS

Joe Simon and Jack Kirby recognized a need for a patriotic figure for America's youth to rally around as the storm clouds of war gathered around Europe. What neither man expected was for Captain America to become a popular icon who has endured for over seventy-five years. This book is a tribute to their genius.

Thanks go to the writers and artists who, for the last eight decades, have populated what is now known as the Marvel Universe, allowing me to mine its rich history for characters, settings, and events to enrich this tale.

More immediately, thanks to Jeff Youngquist, Tom Brevoort, and Axel Alonso at Marvel Comics for their support. A nod to fellow International Association of Media Tie-In Writers pal Matt Forbeck (with help from Alan Cowsill and Daniel Wallace) for his excellent *Captain America: The Ultimate Guide to the First Avenger*, which became a well-thumbed-thorough resource. The two-volume *Marvel Atlas* from 2007 was also the travel guide that helped inform much of the novel's settings.

My first editor, Michael Melgaard, was a constant champion of the story and made substantive contributions to make it a better tale. Joe Books's jack-of-all-trades, Deanna McFadden, stepped in to complete the project and provided thoughtful feedback and solid constructive criticism, putting up with endless questions and comments. My appreciation to both.

My trio of beta readers—Jim Beard, John Trumbull, and especially Paul Simpson—volunteered their time and helped make this a stronger novel. Their input was invaluable and all errors remain of my own making.

And of course, none of this would be possible without the enduring support and encouragement of my wife Deb.

ABOUT THE AUTHOR

Robert Greenberger is a writer and editor. A lifelong fan of comic books, comic strips, science fiction, and *Star Trek*, he drifted toward writing and editing, encouraged by his father and inspired by Superman's alter ego, Clark Kent.

While at SUNY-Binghamton, Greenberger wrote and edited for the college newspaper, *Pipe Dream*. Upon graduation, he worked for Starlog Press and while there, created *Comics Scene*, the first nationally distributed magazine to focus on comic books, comic strips, and animation.

In 1984, he joined DC Comics as an assistant editor, and went on to be an editor before moving to administration as manager, editorial operations. Greenberger joined Gist Communications as a producer before moving to Marvel Comics as its director, publishing operations.

Greenberger rejoined DC in May 2002 as a senior editor, collected editions. He helped grow that department, introducing new formats, and improving the editions' editorial content. In 2006, he joined *Weekly World News* as its managing editor until the paper's untimely demise. He then freelanced for an extensive client base including Platinum Studios, scifi.com, DC, and Marvel. He helped revitalize *Famous Monsters of Filmland* and served as news editor at ComicMix.com.

He is a member of the Science Fiction Writers of America and the International Association of Media Tie-In Writers. His novelization of *Hellboy II: The Golden Army* won the IAMTW's Scribe Award in 2009.

In 2012, Greenberger received his Master of Science in Education from the University of Bridgeport and relocated to Maryland, where he taught high-school English in Baltimore County. He completed his Master of Arts in Creative Writing & Literature for Educators at Fairleigh Dickinson University in 2016.

With others, Greenberger cofounded Crazy 8 Press, a digital press hub where he continues to write. He's also one of the dozen authors using the pen name Rowan Casey to write the Veil Knights urban fantasy series. His dozens of books, short stories, and essays cover the gamut from young adult nonfiction to original fiction.

Greenberger and his wife Deborah reside in Howard County, Maryland, where he teaches high-school English at St. Vincent Pallotti High School. Find him at *www.bobgreenberger.com* or @bobgreenberger.